Jack and Kitty's Christmas Feel-Good Stories

Holidays in the Heartland

Jack Norton

Kitty Norton

Contents

Foreword by Santa Claus

Ho Ho Ho! Merry Christmas, dear readers!

I'm Santa Claus, coming to you from the twinkling lights and joyful hustle of the North Pole. As I sit here, sipping on a cup of Mrs. Claus's famous hot cocoa (she sends her warmest regards, by the way!), I can't help but feel a special kind of excitement. Why, you ask? Because I have the delightful honor of introducing you to "Jack and Kitty's Christmas Feel-Good Stories: Holidays in the Heartland".

Now, you might think that up here in the North Pole, we're too busy with our lists and toy-making to read. But let me tell you, Jack and Kitty's book has become a bit of a sensation among my elves and reindeer. Why, even Rudolph's nose glows a tad brighter when we read their heartwarming tales!

This book, my friends, is a collection of stories that will tug at your heartstrings and tickle your funny bones. Jack and Kitty, those Emmy Award-winning travel experts from Minnesota, have outdone themselves. They've woven a tapestry of holiday cheer and Midwest charm that's as comforting as a warm blanket on a snowy evening.

As you turn each page, you'll find yourself on a magical sleigh ride through the wonders of the festive season. From quirky traditions to heartfelt moments, these stories are a celebration of what makes the holidays truly special. And trust me, after centuries of delivering presents, I know a thing or two about the magic of Christmas!

So, snuggle up by the fireplace, pour yourself some hot cider, and prepare to be whisked away on a festive journey. Mrs. Claus, the elves, the reindeer, and I are all thrilled to share the joy of "Jack and Kitty's Christmas Feel-Good Stories: Holidays in the Heartland" with you.

Merry reading, and may your holidays be as merry and bright as a star on a Christmas tree!

With jolly wishes,
Santa Claus
North Pole

Chapter 1

Joyful Jingle

Once upon a snowy evening in the twinkling town of Falls City, Nebraska, Ellie, a shy girl with a heart full of dreams, stood quietly in the corner of her cozy living room. Unlike her siblings, Ellie had never found her musical talent. While Braydon excelled at the guitar and Savanah's voice could charm birds from the trees, Ellie felt lost in their melodious shadows.

This year, their parents had signed them up to join a local Christmas caroling group.

Ellie was horrified by her parent's announcement.

The thought of joining the caroling group filled her with dread. She couldn't bear the thought of standing amidst the chorus, the only one silent, her lack of musical ability exposed for all to see. Her shyness made the idea of hiding away far more appealing than facing the embarrassment.

Her older siblings, Braydon and Savanah, were bustling around, gathering scarves and gloves for the evening's caroling. Ellie, with her quiet voice and introverted nature, felt overshadowed by their exuberance and talents.

"Ellie, aren't you coming caroling?" Braydon asked, his voice echoing with excitement.

She shook her head, her eyes downcast. "I don't think I'll be any good at it."

Savanah, tying her scarf, chimed in, "Oh, come on, Ellie! It's Christmas. It's about being together, not about being perfect."

Ellie's mom, noticing her hesitation, walked over with a warm smile. "You know, Ellie, sometimes the smallest things can make the biggest difference. Why don't you bring those old jingle bells from the Christmas tree? They might add a nice touch to our songs."

With a hesitant nod, Ellie picked up the old, slightly tarnished jingle bells, their gentle tinkle bringing a small smile to her face. The jingle bells, sewn onto on a pretty green velvet ribbon, had always been one of her favorite tree ornaments.

Even if I don't want to be here, at least I can hold the soft ribbon in my hand, Ellie thought to herself. *And maybe it will help me to feel a little less nervous.* With the ribbon of jingle bells clutched between her fingers, Ellie and her family left the house.

As the caroling group wandered through the snow-dusted streets, singing joyously, Ellie stayed at the back, the jingle bells held tightly in her hands. At each house, Braydon and Savanah's voices rang out strong and clear, while Ellie's remained a silent whisper.

Then, as they approached the town's nursing home, Ellie felt a tug at her heart. The residents, wrapped in blankets, were gathered in the main entryway, their eyes reflecting the twinkling Christmas lights.

"Let's sing 'Silent Night'," suggested Braydon. The group

agreed, and as the first notes floated in the air, Ellie, almost without thinking, started to shake the jingle bells. The soft, melodic sound blended perfectly with the voices, adding a magical layer to the song.

The residents' faces lit up, their smiles wide and genuine. Ellie, feeling their joy, played with more confidence, her shyness melting away with each shake of the bells.

After the song, an elderly lady beckoned Ellie over. "My dear, your bells... they reminded me of a Christmas long ago. You have a special talent for bringing joy," she said, her eyes glistening.

Ellie's heart swelled with happiness. For the first time, she felt seen, not for being the loudest or the most noticeable, but for adding a subtle, yet beautiful, harmony to the world.

As they walked back home, her family showered her with compliments. "Ellie, you were amazing!" Savanah exclaimed.

Braydon added, "You should play those bells every year!"

That night, as Ellie lay in bed, the jingle bells by her side, she realized the true magic of Christmas. It wasn't about being the best; it was about bringing joy in your own unique way. And for Ellie, that was the most heartwarming gift of all.

"There are no strangers here; only friends you haven't met yet."

William Butler Yeats

Chapter 2

Fifty Winters of Hope

In the small, snow-dusted town of Tomah, Wisconsin, Clara, a gentle-hearted librarian, found a mysterious package in her mailbox on a crisp December morning. It looked battered and dirty, with no return address. Taking a closer look, Clara could see faded postal stamps on the back, written in a foreign language.

With care, Clara opened the anonymous package. Inside was a thick, weathered envelope, its surface adorned with ink and postal stamps in various languages. The old, yellowed envelope appeared as though it had passed through countless hands over the years. Carefully, to avoid tearing it, she gently extracted its contents.

Clara gasped in awe. Inside was a bundle of papers of different sizes and styles, all bound with a faded red ribbon. Each sheet bore a heartwarming message or story, reflective of its writer's life. Some letters even featured hand-drawn pictures from children.

Clara scanned through the handwritten messages,

amazed. One of the oldest messages was written over 50 years ago! In her hands was a collection of touching Christmas letters, each penned by someone from a different corner of the globe.

But the shocking part was the latest letter, addressed to her:

Dear Clara,

We hope this letter finds its way to you and greets you with warmth and happiness. Though we've never met, and your name and address came to us through a search online, we felt compelled to reach out in the spirit of connection and goodwill.

This year has brought unexpected changes for our family. Just yesterday, Damon, my husband, returned home with the heavy news of losing his job. It was a moment that could have darkened our spirits, but we've chosen to look for light in these trying times...

The letter continued on, giving Clara a glimpse of the Jones family's daily life in sunny Australia. As she read, Clara felt as if she'd known this precious family her entire life, the letter forging a connection in her heart that seemed impossible from one handwritten letter.

The beautiful message ended on a hopeful note, with the entire family signing it, even the family's cat leaving a paw print in colorful paint. Clara chuckled, wiping a tear that escaped from her eye. This mysterious package was a gift, showing her how a simple act of sharing can bring the world a little closer.

Each evening after work, wrapped in her coziest blanket,

Clara immersed herself in these letters. They weren't just words; they were windows into the lives of others, brimming with stories of personal struggle, hope and dreams. From a fisherman in Greece sharing tales of the sea to a teacher in Kenya speaking of the joy in her students' eyes, each letter was a tribute to the human spirit.

Her best friend, Stephanie, a fellow librarian with a love for stories, joined Clara at home one evening. "This is amazing," she exclaimed, her eyes sparkling as she read through the letters. "I can't believe all these people took time to write these thoughtful letters. And from so many places, too!"

"It's extraordinary, isn't it?" Clara said. "It's like holding hands with the world." Clara looked at the letters for a moment, her heart full. She knew it was time to add her contribution to the bundle. "This year, it's my turn to keep this legacy going."

The thought both excited and daunted her. She wanted her message to resonate with warmth and sincerity, to be a glimmer of hope in the ever-growing chain of goodwill.

That evening, Clara hosted a small gathering at her home for her coworkers from the library and their families. The children's librarian and her husband, who had just adopted a little boy from Bolivia named Afonso, were among the guests. The couple lovingly tended to Afonso, ensuring he felt welcome in his new environment. Afonso's mom, intrigued by Clara's bundle of letters from around the world, inquired about them.

"So these letters come from everywhere?" she asked.

"Yes, we even have one from Antarctica!" Clara replied, her voice filled with excitement.

Afonso's mom paused, her eyes alight with thought.

"This gives me an idea," she said. "When we visited Afonso's orphanage, the stories there touched my heart. These letters... I think we could do something to help."

She explained that Afonso's village was impoverished and the orphanage struggled to meet its needs. The local adoption agency in Bolivia, which had facilitated Afonso's adoption, was always in need of support.

"Why don't we all write messages for the kids at the orphanage and collect funds to send to them? We can include them in this bundle of letters," she suggested.

The library staff enthusiastically embraced the idea. They sat down together, each penning a message of love and encouragement, and made pledges to gather more donations in the coming days.

After the guests had left and the house had quieted down, Clara sat to write her letter. Inspired by the day's events, she wrote about the power of unexpected connections and the joy found in simple acts of kindness.

At the end of the week, Clara handed the envelope and its contents to Afonso's mom. "Take this with you," she said, her voice soft. "And next Christmas, have the orphanage pass the letters on. I've included a little extra money for postage so that this chain of love can continue."

Afonso's mom was moved. "We'll cherish this," she promised, her eyes shining with gratitude.

Clara watched her leave, the package in her hands, ready to travel to another corner of the world. She felt a profound sense of peace, knowing her words and gift would soon touch another heart, in a place she might never see.

As she sat in silence, watching the snowflakes dance in the moonlight, Clara realized her spirit felt lighter than it had in years. She smiled, knowing deep down she had made a difference. Through that mysterious package that arrived a week ago, she understood a profound truth: Love knows no boundaries and can be spread in many ways—sometimes through one letter, one story, one heart at a time.

Chapter 3

A Fitting Ring for Madison

Diego grew up in an unassuming neighborhood in Williamsburg, Iowa. Still in graduate school, he wanted to show the love of his life, Madison, how much she meant to him. His greatest wish was to propose to Madison with a ring as radiant as her happy smile. But, working tirelessly in a small diner between classes, Diego could only save enough for a modest yet pretty ring from the local antique store, far from the diamond he dreamed of giving her.

On a chilly December evening, Diego nervously pocketed the delicate ring, a glimmer of hope in his heart. He planned to propose under the grand Christmas tree in the town square, where they had first met.

As they walked hand in hand, Madison's eyes lit up at the sight of the tree, its lights twinkling like stars. "It's beautiful, isn't it, Diego?" she said, her breath visible in the frosty air.

Diego's heart pounded. "Madison, you make every moment beautiful," he began, his voice trembling. He got down on his knees. "I may not have much, but I have a heart full of love for you. Will you marry me?" He presented the ring with a hopeful smile.

Madison's eyes filled with tears as she nodded. "Yes, Diego, I will. Your love is all I need."

The next day, the couple took the ring to the local jeweler to get it resized for Madison's finger. The jeweler was an elderly man, who was nearing retirement.

Diego, embarrassed by the modesty of his ring compared to the fancy ones displayed in the cases, offered a humble apology. "I know this ring isn't much, but Madison here has agreed to marry me, and one day I'll buy her the most expensive ring in this store!"

"Diego, this ring is perfect as it is," Madison interrupted. "I don't need an expensive one to know how much you love me," Madison's eyes were shining with affection as she admired the modest ring on her finger.

"Engaged, huh? Well, congratulations to you both!" The jeweler smiled at Madison and Diego. "This is a fine ring you've chosen. May I take a closer look?"

The jeweler inspected it closely, his eyes widening in surprise. "Remarkable! This is a rare design from the early 1900s, one I've never before seen in person. It's *quite* valuable."

Diego and Madison gasped in disbelief as the man explained the history and worth of the ring.

As the jeweler shared the surprising history of the ring, Madison's eyes widened in astonishment. "Oh my goodness!" she gasped, her hand flying to her mouth. "It's not just beautiful, but it has its own story too!"

"The magic of Christmas must be at work today," the

man chuckled. "What you thought was a simple ring is actually a treasure."

Overwhelmed with joy, Diego and Madison embraced, their hearts brimming with love and the unexpected fortune of their engagement ring. Madison smiled brightly, her eyes alight with love and excitement. "See? I told you it was perfect. I wouldn't trade this ring for anything in the world."

As they walked home, snow gently falling around them, the lights of the Christmas tree seemed to shine even brighter, reflecting the magical turn their lives had just taken.

As far as Diego was concerned, the universe had his back. He knew he wasn't the wealthiest man on earth, but he was certainly the luckiest.

Madison was going to be his wife. And on their wedding day, when they walked down the aisle and pledged their love forever, Madison would be wearing the beautiful ring she deserved.

"I wonder if the snow loves the trees and fields, that it kisses them so gently?"

Lewis Carroll

Chapter 4

A Dream of Snowflakes

In the warm sands of the Middle East, a young soldier named Ben huddled in his barracks, clutching a crumpled photo of his home in Minnesota. "I miss the snow," he whispered to his bunkmate, Mike, who was busy polishing his boots.

"Snow? You're crazy," Mike chuckled. "It's 100 degrees out here."

"But it's Christmas, Mike. Back home, the world is white, pure, and peaceful," Ben sighed, his eyes distant.

The days rolled on, each blending into the next under the relentless sun. But Ben's yearning for a white Christmas only grew stronger. He shared stories of Minnesota winters with anyone who would listen: the snowball fights, the silent, snow-covered streets, and the warmth of family gatherings.

On Christmas Eve, the base was abuzz with a subdued festive spirit. Soldiers exchanged makeshift gifts and stories of Christmases past. As the night deepened, Ben found himself outside, staring at the starry sky.

"I'd give anything for a bit of snow," he murmured.

Suddenly, Mike appeared beside him, a mischievous glint in his eye. "Follow me," he said.

Curious, Ben trailed Mike to a secluded part of the base. There, to his astonishment, was a small pile of white, fluffy... snow?

"How?" Ben gasped.

Mike grinned. "Let's just say I have my connections. It's not much, but..."

It was more than enough. For a moment, Ben was transported back to Minnesota. He scooped up a handful of snow, letting it fall through his fingers. Tears welled in his eyes, not just for the snow, but for the gesture, the friendship, the touch of home in a faraway land.

That night, as Ben lay in his bunk, a soft peace settled over him. It wasn't the Christmas he had dreamed of, but it was a Christmas he would never forget, a reminder of the magic of human connection, even in the most unlikely places.

"Merry Christmas, Ben," Mike whispered from the other side of the room.

"Merry Christmas, Mike. And thank you," Ben replied, a smile on his face, as he drifted off to sleep, dreaming of snowflakes and the warmth of home.

Just for Laughs!

A gingerbread man went to the doctor's complaining of a sore knee. The doctor asked him. "Have you tried icing it?"

Chapter 5

The Gingerbread Bake-Off

The holiday season was in full swing in East Grand Forks, Minnesota. In the middle of town stood a warm, cozy bakery owned by Lauren Schmidt. The scent of spices and freshly baked treats filled the air. The bakery, with its quaint decor and welcoming vibe, was a local favorite, especially during the holidays.

Izzy Schmidt, Lauren's ten-year-old daughter, watched her mother with wide, admiring eyes. Lauren was in her element, moving around the kitchen with practiced ease, her hands skillfully shaping dough into gingerbread cookies.

"Mom, they're perfect!" Izzy exclaimed, her voice a mixture of awe and excitement.

Lauren smiled, brushing a stray lock of hair from her forehead with the back of her hand. "Thank you, sweetie. But remember, baking is not just about being perfect. It's about putting your heart into what you make."

Izzy nodded, her eyes following every movement of her mother's hands. "I want to try too. I want to be in the junior baking competition this year."

Lauren turned to Izzy, her expression a blend of surprise and delight. "Really? That's a wonderful idea! But it's a lot of hard work, you know?"

Izzy's face lit up with determination. "I know, Mom. But I want to make gingerbread man cookies and a parfait, just like you!"

Over the next few days, the bakery became a hub of activity and learning for Izzy. She was determined to master the art of baking, just like her mother. Lauren showed her how to mix ingredients, roll out dough, and the delicate art of baking the perfect gingerbread cookie.

One evening, as they were cleaning up, Izzy looked up at her mother. "Do you think I can really do it, Mom? Win the competition, I mean?"

Lauren put down the cloth she was holding and knelt down to Izzy's level. "Winning isn't what's important, Izzy. What matters is that you try your best and have fun. Remember, it's all about the joy of creating something and sharing it with others."

Izzy nodded, a thoughtful expression on her face. "I guess you're right, Mom. It's just that... I want to make you proud."

Lauren hugged her tightly. "Izzy, you make me proud every day. Just by being you."

The next morning, East Grand Forks awoke to a flurry of excitement. The annual holiday baking competition was just a week away, and the town was buzzing with anticipation. Izzy had been practicing recipes with every spare moment she had. For Izzy, it wasn't just a baking competition, it was her first big step towards her dream.

One day she wanted to run a famous bakery, just like her mom.

In the bakery's kitchen, Izzy stood in front of a bowl of dough, her brow furrowed in concentration. She was trying to remember the exact sequence her mother had shown her. "Okay, so I mix the flour with the spices first, then add the molasses..." she muttered to herself.

Lauren watched from a distance, her heart swelling with pride and a touch of amusement. "Remember to add the baking soda, Izzy. It'll help the cookies rise."

"Oh, right!" Izzy exclaimed, quickly adding the forgotten ingredient.

The first batch of cookies came out of the oven hard as rocks. Izzy's face fell as she tapped one with her spoon, hearing a distinct 'clink.' "Mom, they're too hard!"

Lauren chuckled, walking over to her. "It's okay, honey. Baking is all about trial and error. Let's try reducing the baking time."

The next attempt was better, but not quite right. The cookies were still too tough, but at least they didn't resemble stones. Izzy refused to be disheartened. "Third time's the charm, right?"

"That's the spirit," Lauren encouraged.

The real challenge, however, came with the gingerbread and ice cream parfait. Izzy had watched her mother create this masterpiece countless times, but doing it herself was another story.

She carefully layered gingerbread crumbs at the bottom of a glass, then added a scoop of homemade vanilla ice cream, followed by a drizzle of caramel sauce. It looked perfect, until the ice cream started to melt, turning the once neat layers into a mushy mixture.

Izzy stared at the parfait, her face a mixture of frustration and humor. "Well, this didn't go as planned."

Lauren couldn't help but laugh. "It's okay, Izzy. Maybe we need to freeze the glasses first to keep the ice cream from melting too fast."

Throughout the week, the bakery's regular customers got to witness Izzy's endeavors. They offered tips, shared their own baking disasters, and encouraged her to keep trying. Mrs. Vang, the elderly lady who came in every morning for a cinnamon roll, patted Izzy's hand and said, "Dear, the best bakers are those who make the most mistakes. You're doing just fine."

Finally, after several more attempts, Izzy managed to bake a batch of gingerbread men cookies that were almost right – a bit uneven in size, with a sloppy appearance that could even be described as ugly...but deliciously soft and spicy. Her parfait, though not as elegant as her mother's, had its own rustic charm.

As they prepared to close the bakery that evening, Lauren put an arm around Izzy's shoulders. "You've done so well, Izzy. No matter what happens tomorrow, you should be proud of yourself."

Izzy looked up at her mother, a determined glint in her eyes. "I am proud, Mom. And I'm ready for the competition. I want to show everyone what I've learned."

The day of the holiday baking competition dawned clear and cold in East Grand Forks. The town hall, where the event was held, buzzed with excitement and the delicious aromas of holiday treats. Izzy, dressed in her favorite apron, stood nervously beside her table, where her gingerbread men cookies and parfait were displayed.

Lauren squeezed her daughter's hand reassuringly. "You've done wonderfully, Izzy. Just look at how many people are admiring your work."

Indeed, several townsfolk were gathered around Izzy's table, smiling and encouraging her for her efforts. Her cookies, though not as uniform as the other entries, had a charming homemade look, and her parfait, while a bit slumped, was inviting.

"Thanks, Mom," Izzy whispered, her eyes scanning the room filled with elaborate cakes and pastries. "But look at all the other entries. They're so... perfect."

Lauren leaned down to whisper in her ear, "Perfection isn't what makes something special, Izzy. It's the love and effort you put into it."

As the judges made their rounds, tasting and noting, Izzy watched with bated breath. The judges smiled and nodded as they sampled her cookies and parfait. Izzy's heart soared; she had done her best, and that was all that mattered.

Suddenly, the lights flickered and went out, plunging the town hall into darkness. Murmurs of confusion rippled through the crowd. Outside, snowflakes began to swirl in a rapidly intensifying snowstorm.

"Oh no, the power's out!" someone shouted.

In the dim light filtering through the windows, Lauren's calm voice could be heard. "Everyone, stay calm. Let's light some candles and make the best of this situation."

As people scrambled to find candles and flashlights, Izzy's table became a small gathering of light and warmth. Her clownish gingerbread cookies, now being passed around, brought smiles to people's faces.

The little imperfections, lovingly crafted with homemade care drew onlookers right to her table. They couldn't help but fall in love with the little girl's enthusiasm, even if the gingerbread men looked oddly engorged and misshapen.

An elderly gentleman, Mr. Christensen, took a bite and

chuckled. "These remind me of my wife's baking. Not perfect to look at, but perfect in taste."

Soon, the town hall was filled with cheerful laughter and stories, as people shared their own holiday memories and experiences. The competition was forgotten; instead, it turned into a spontaneous holiday gathering, with Izzy's cookies and parfait at the center of it all.

Amidst the encouraging laughter and shared stories, Lauren looked at Izzy, her eyes shining with pride. "See, Izzy? This is what the holidays are all about. Coming together, sharing, and enjoying the simple things."

Izzy, watching the joy her baking had brought to the community, felt a warmth spread through her. She may not have won a trophy, but she had won something much more valuable – the love and appreciation of her community.

As the snowstorm raged outside, the people of East Grand Forks celebrated inside, united by the holiday spirit and the unexpected joy brought about by a little girl's baking. The competition ended without a formal announcement of winners, but for Izzy and the people of her town, it was a night they would always remember.

As they finally made their way home, Izzy looked up at the falling snow and said, "Mom, this was the best holiday ever. I feel like I did win, in a way."

Lauren hugged her tightly. "You did win, Izzy. You won our hearts. You're my little holiday miracle."

"Be yourself; everyone else is already taken."

Oscar Wilde

Chapter 6

Brewing Love

The crisp air of October and the colorful hues of Autumn leaves had turned Waverly, Iowa into a cozy oasis. The lights from charming storefronts on Brewer Avenue cast a warm glow over the quaint town. In a small, charming coffee shop, Zoe, a college freshman, steamed milk for a latte. She was lost in thoughts about her upcoming exam and daydreams of traveling far beyond the bounds of Iowa.

The bell above the door jingled, signaling the arrival of a customer. Zoe looked up and was met with the sight of a tall, handsome man shaking a stray leaf from his dark hair. He wore a warm smile that lit up his eyes.

"Hi, a cappuccino, please," he said, his voice friendly and inviting.

"Sure thing," Zoe replied, feeling a flutter of nerves. "You're not from around here, are you?" He looked sophisticated, and his dark clothes looked expensive and stylish. Too stylish for a small town like Waverly.

"No, just visiting a friend for a while," he answered, his

eyes scanning the array of pastries. "I'm Caleb."

"I'm Zoe. So, a cappuccino and... anything else?" Zoe asked, trying to sound casual.

Caleb pointed at a cinnamon roll. "That looks good. Are they your specialty?"

Zoe chuckled. "I wish. I just serve them. But I can vouch for their deliciousness."

As Zoe prepared the order, they made small talk for a few minutes. Caleb talked about his travels, and his love for classic literature. Zoe shared dreams of seeing the world after graduation. They laughed over a few of Waverly's small town quirks.

"There you go," Zoe said, handing over the cappuccino and cinnamon roll. "I hope it tastes as good as it looks."

"I'm sure it will. Thanks, Zoe. Maybe I'll see you around?" Caleb said, with a hopeful note in his voice.

Zoe was secretly flattered that he'd remembered her name. "Maybe," she replied, feeling a warm surge of excitement. "Enjoy Waverly!"

As Caleb walked away, Zoe couldn't help but smile. The rest of the evening passed in a blur, the encounter replaying in Zoe's mind.

Over the next few weeks, Caleb became a regular. Zoe started planning her shift breaks around his visits so they had more time to talk. Each visit brought new stories and laughter, deepening the connection between them. Zoe looked forward to these moments, finding joy in Caleb's company amidst the stress of college life. It was more than just attraction; it was a genuine connection that felt rare and precious.

As December approached, and the town readied for the Holiday Season, Zoe found herself dreaming of Caleb more and more often. She realized that these moments with Caleb were becoming the highlight of her day. It wasn't just the sparkle of Waverly's Christmas lights that brought warmth to Zoe's heart; it was the unexpected joy of getting to know someone who made the ordinary feel extraordinary.

The December days shortened and Waverly's streets glowed with festive lights, Zoe and Caleb's friendship blossomed. They shared stories over steaming cups of coffee, their laughter echoing in the cozy confines of the coffee shop. Occasionally, they strolled through the snow-covered streets, admiring the holiday decorations and the serene beauty of the winter nights.

One chilly evening, as they walked along the Cedar River, Zoe ventured, "Caleb, you talk about so many places, but you never mention where you're from."

Caleb's eyes flickered with a hint of mystery. "I guess I'm a bit of a wanderer. Home is wherever inspiration takes me," he said, changing the subject to the twinkling lights on the river.

Zoe, smitten and intrigued, didn't press further. There was something about Caleb that felt like a puzzle waiting to be solved, but the comfort of his presence was enough for Zoe.

A week before Christmas, the air in town was filled with anticipation. Caleb walked into the coffee shop, his expression a mix of joy and sadness. Zoe felt a tug of worry.

"I have something to tell you," Caleb began hesitantly, as they sat down with their usual coffee orders.

"What is it?" Zoe asked, a knot forming in her stomach.

"I need to leave Waverly for a while," Caleb said, his eyes not meeting Zoe's. "There's something I must take care of. I promise I'll explain everything when I come back."

The news hit Zoe like a cold wave. "When will you be

back?"

"I don't know yet."

Tears brimmed in Zoe's eyes. She didn't want Caleb to see her so upset, but she couldn't help it. They had just started to get really close, and now he was leaving. "When do you leave?"

Caleb smiled sadly. "Tomorrow evening. But I'll swing through to say goodbye before I leave, I promise."

"Wow, tomorrow...that's so soon." Zoe tried to hide the disappointment in her voice. "Okay. I'll see you tomorrow then." She was certain Caleb could see the sadness in her eyes in spite of her smile.

The next day came and went, with no sign of Caleb.

Zoe heart sunk with each moment that passed. Little did she know, Caleb *did* come to say goodbye, but not in the way she assumed.

As the evening fell into shadows, Caleb stood outside the coffee shop, watching Zoe through the window. He watched her greet the customers, admiring the way her smile lit up the room. He longed to go inside, to say goodbye, but the words wouldn't come.

So he did the only thing he knew to do. He watched her. For almost two hours.

Unable to leave yet, Caleb braved the cold wind and watched her until her shift ended. From the cover of a tree, Caleb watched Zoe as she walked out of the coffee shop and out of his life forever.

Caleb's heart ached with the weight of unspoken love. He hadn't realized just how much he'd fallen for Zoe until it was time to say goodbye. With a heavy heart, he turned and walked away.

After Caleb's sudden departure, the coffee shop felt

emptier to Zoe. She picked up extra shifts at the coffee shop, hoping that if she stayed busy enough, she'd stop thinking about him and all the little moments they'd shared together.

The hours turned into almost a week, and still no word from Caleb. Zoe was devastated by his rejection. At least, she was telling herself it was simply rejection, and not something far worse.

She couldn't bear the thought of something bad happening to Caleb. She hoped he was safe, wherever he was.

On Christmas Eve morning, Zoe was working her last shift before Christmas Break. A gentle snowfall painted Waverly's streets in serene whites and soft grays. Zoe, surrounded by festive decorations, was lost in thoughts of Caleb.

Each jingle of the doorbell still brought a hopeful glance, quickly fading to disappointment as familiar faces, not Caleb's, came into view.

Zoe decided to give up hope of ever seeing Caleb again. She was determined to not let his selfishness ruin her Christmas. To tell the truth, Zoe was angry and more than a little hurt by his behavior. She absentmindedly arranged a fresh batch of gingerbread cookies, when the bell chimed again.

Zoe looked up and gasped out loud. There stood Caleb, his eyes alight with an emotion Zoe couldn't quite place.

"Caleb!" Zoe's voice was a mix of surprise, concern and hope. "What are you doing here?"

"I had to come back," Caleb said, his voice steady and sincere. "Merry Christmas, Zoe."

"But why? I thought you were gone...you didn't say good-bye..." Zoe's words trailed off, a hopeful note rising in their voice.

Caleb took a step closer, his gaze unwavering. "I did leave, but not for the reasons you might think. I'm a writer, Zoe, and I came to Waverly looking for inspiration for my novel. I submitted my manuscript, and was going back home to Manhattan. But then I realized something."

"What did you realize?" Zoe asked, heart racing.

"That I've fallen in love with you, Zoe. I was supposed to leave Waverly for good after my book was submitted. But I couldn't. I now this might sound crazy, but I haven't been able to get you out of my head since I left. I don't want to be anywhere else but here, with you," Caleb confessed, his eyes shining with emotion.

The revelation took Zoe's breath away. "You love me?"

"More than I thought possible," Caleb affirmed. "These past couple of months, getting to know you, sharing stories and dreams, it's changed me. I want to be here, in Waverly, if you'll have me."

The coffee shop door opened, and a couple of regulars began to trickle in, getting a cup cheer before their holiday festivities began. But for Zoe, the world had narrowed down to this moment, to Caleb and his heartfelt confession.

"I... I don't know what to say," Zoe stammered, joy mingling with disbelief.

"Say you'll let me stay. Say you feel something for me too," Caleb said, reaching for Zoe's hand.

Zoe looked into Caleb's eyes, seeing the truth and love reflected there. "Yes, I feel it too. I want you to stay."

The coffee shop was busy with Christmas greetings and festive chatter, but Zoe and Caleb were in a world of their own, wrapped in the magic of the moment. They knew this was more than just a holiday romance. It was the beginning of a beautiful journey together.

Just for Laughs!

from JackAndKitty.com

What brand of motorcycle does Santa ride? Holly Davidson.

Chapter 7

'Twas the Night Before Christmas...in Iowa

Here's a silly take on the classic Christmas poem, served with an extra dish of corn for our friends in Iowa!

* * *

'Twas the night before Christmas, all over the farm,
Not a piglet was squealing, causing no alarm;
The stockings were hung by the chimney just so,
In hopes that Saint Nick would bring new tractor glow;

The children were snoozing, all cozy in spreads,
With visions of cornfields swaying in their heads;
And mamma in her kerchief, and I in my cap,
Had just settled in for a long winter's nap,

When out on the pasture there came such a racket,
I sprang from the bed, pulling on my jacket.
Away to the window I stumbled in stride,

Tore open the shutters, and threw the pane wide.

The moon shone on silos and snow-speckled corn,
Giving a luster as bright as the morn,
When, what to my wondering eyes should draw near,
But a John Deere sleigh, and eight chunky reindeer,

With a little old driver, so lively and quick,
I knew in a flash it had to be Saint Nick.
More rapid than pheasants his coursers they came,
And he whistled, and shouted, and called them by name:

"Now, Maizey! now, Beans! now, Plow and Milker!
On, Combine! on, Silo! on, Donner and Tiller!
To the top of the barn! to the top of the wall!
Now dash away! dash away! dash away all!"

As leaves that before the wild prairie fly,
When they meet an obstacle, mount to the sky;
So up to the farmhouse-top the coursers they flew,
With a sleigh full of gifts, and Saint Nicholas too.

And then, in a twinkling, I heard on the roof
The prancing and pawing of each little hoof.
As I drew in my head, and was turning around,
Down the chimney Saint Nicholas came with a bound.

He was dressed all in denim, from his head to his toe,
With a vest patched with quilt squares and a warm, flannel
glow;
A bundle of toys he had flung on his back,
He looked like a peddler just opening his pack.

His eyes—how they sparkled! his dimples, how merry!
His cheeks were like roses, his nose like a cherry!
His droll little mouth was drawn up like a bow,
And the beard of his chin was as white as the snow.

The stump of an ear of corn he held tight in his grin,
And the butter it melted right down to his chin;
He had a broad face and a round little belly,
That shook when he chuckled, like a bowlful of jelly.

He was chubby and plump, a right jolly old man,
And I laughed when I saw him—because I'm a fan;
A wink of his eye and a twist of his head
Soon gave me to know I had nothing to dread;

He spoke not a word, but went straight to his duty,
Filling all the stockings with toys and some beauty.
And laying his finger aside of his nose,
And giving a nod, up the chimney he rose;

He sprang to his sleigh, to his team gave a holler,
And away they all flew, like a dollar for a scholar.
But I heard him exclaim, as he drove out of sight,
"Happy Christmas to Iowa, and to all a good-night!"

"May you never be too grown up to search the skies on Christmas Eve."

Unknown

Chapter 8

A Heartfelt Christmas Tree

Once in a small, cozy apartment in the heart of a Kansas City, Missouri there lived a young boy named Felix and his mother, Wanda. Felix, with his bright eyes and boundless imagination, was the light of Wanda's world. Every day after school, Felix would return to their humble abode, where a simple dinner awaited him in the fridge, lovingly prepared by Wanda before she left for her second job.

Felix, a self-reliant little boy, had grown accustomed to looking after himself in the evenings, as his mom couldn't afford childcare. He didn't mind though; the television provided endless adventures, and his teddy bears were always there, offering silent, comforting company until his mommy's return.

Felix admired his mommy immensely, believing she was the hardest worker in the entire world, and he aspired to be just as brave as her when he grew up.

On a chilly December evening, as the first snowflakes of the season drifted lazily outside, Felix sat cross-legged in front of their old, artificial Christmas tree. The tree, barren of decorations or gifts beneath it, seemed to mirror the emptiness they often felt during the holiday season. But this year, Felix decided, would be different.

With determination, he gathered old newspapers, scissors, a box of crayons, and a spool of thread. His small hands worked tirelessly, coloring and cutting the paper, transforming them into vibrant, makeshift ornaments. While working, he turned to his teddy bears lined up beside him.

"Beary Potter, what do you think of this one?" Felix held up a brightly colored ornament, his eyes seeking approval from his stuffed companion.

The teddy bear, with its worn-out fur and friendly eyes, seemed to nod in agreement. Encouraged, Felix continued, chatting with his teddy bears as he worked. "And this one, Mrs. Fluffy, is going to be the star of the tree!" he declared, holding a crudely crayon-colored star.

Mrs. Fluffy, a small bear with a missing eye that Felix had had since he was a baby, sat quietly, a familiar and gentle smile on her face.

He found pairs of his socks, drawing smiling faces on each, and hung them alongside his paper creations. Finally, he lined the bottom of the tree with all of his teddy bears and dinosaur toys, a stand-in for the gifts they couldn't afford.

That night, as Wanda returned home, weary from a long day's work, Felix waited eagerly by the tree. Her eyes, heavy with the fatigue of life's burdens, widened in surprise and then filled with tears as she took in the sight before her.

"Mommy, look! I made us a Christmas tree," Felix exclaimed, his voice filled with pride.

Wanda knelt beside him, her heart swelling with love

and emotion. "Felix, this is the most beautiful tree I have ever seen. How did you...?"

"I wanted to make you happy, mommy. I didn't want you to be sad about not having a bunch of gifts or fancy decorations," Felix said, his eyes shining with innocence and love.

Wanda embraced him tightly, whispering, "You are the greatest gift I could ever ask for, sweetie."

That Christmas, Wanda and Felix learned that the true magic of the season didn't come from the grandest gifts or the most lavish decorations. It came from the heart, from the simple acts of love and kindness that bind us all. And in their little apartment, the spirit of Christmas shone brighter than ever before.

Chapter 9

Baby Jesus Sleeps

In a humble manger, under starlit skies,
Lies a newborn babe, with closed, peaceful eyes.
Surrounded by warmth in the cool night air,
Shepherds and wise men find him there.

Angels sing softly, a heavenly sound,
Proclaiming joy and grace that abound.
In this simple stable, love's pure light,
Baby Jesus sleeps, serene and bright.

Chapter 10

The Night Baby Jesus Listened

In the heart of Rapid City, South Dakota a quaint house twinkled with the warmth of Christmas. Inside, a family of three, soon to be four, shared their lives. The dining room, adorned with a small nativity scene, stood as a testimony of their faith and hope.

One frosty evening, as whispers of winter danced through the air, Seth, the father, was stirred from his slumber. A soft light seeped under the door, drawing him to the dining room. There, he found his young son, Jackson, kneeling by the nativity scene, his small hands clasped in prayer.

"Dear Baby Jesus," Jackson's voice was a gentle murmur, "please keep my mommy and baby sister safe. I promise to be the best big brother."

Seth, touched by the scene, approached softly. "Jackson, it's late, buddy. What are you doing up?"

Jackson looked up, his eyes bright with innocence. "I was talking to Baby Jesus, Daddy. I asked him to look after Mommy and the baby."

Seth knelt beside his son, enveloped in the purity of the moment. "That's very kind of you, Jackson. I'm sure Baby Jesus heard your prayer."

As they spoke, a gentle gust of wind rattled the windows, drawing their attention to a peculiar sight outside. A single, bright star seemed to glow unusually vivid in the night sky, casting a serene light over their home.

"Look, Daddy, it's like the Christmas Star!" Jackson exclaimed, his face alight with wonder.

Seth hugged his son. "Yes, it is. Just like the one that guided the Wise Men."

In that instant, a cry echoed through the house. Umm, Seth... you better come here, I think my water just broke!'

In the heart of their cozy home, organized chaos erupted. Seth, with a mix of excitement and urgency, called his mother. "Mom, it's time," he said, his voice tinged with anticipation.

He then assisted his wife, Bethany, who was cradling her swollen belly. "Are you ready, love?" he asked gently.

Bethany nodded, a nervous smile on her face. "As ready as I'll ever be," she replied.

Seth swiftly grabbed their pre-packed suitcase, assisting Bethany to their minivan. Within minutes, they were en route to the hospital, meeting Jackson's grandmother there.

In the hospital waiting room, Jackson sat with his grandmother, a bundle of nervous energy. She bought him juice and potato chips from a vending machine, trying to keep his spirits up. "Here you go, sweetheart. These should tide you over," she said, handing him the snacks.

Jackson nibbled absent-mindedly, his eyes glued to the videos playing on his grandmother's phone. Time seemed to crawl. His eyelids grew heavy, and he leaned against his grandmother, fighting sleep. "Grandma, do you think they'll be okay?" he mumbled, his voice laced with concern.

"Of course, Jackson. Everything will be just fine," she reassured him, stroking his hair gently.

Eventually, Seth emerged, looking weary but hopeful. "It's taking a bit longer than we thought," he explained. "You two should head home and get some rest."

Back at home, Jackson was tucked into bed by his grandmother. But sleep eluded him. In the quiet of the night, he got out of his bed and made his way to the nativity scene in the dining room. He whispered a prayer, his small hands clasped tightly. "Baby Jesus, I know you're watching over my mommy and baby sister," he murmured, his voice full of hope.

The next day, after a prolonged labor, joyous news arrived. A healthy baby girl, 7 pounds 6 ounces. They named her Hazel, and she was a sight to behold.

Jackson's grandmother took him to see Hazel at the hospital. He peered at her through the big glass window, marveling at her tiny form. "She's so little," he whispered in awe.

Finally, the awaited day arrived. Hazel was coming home. As Seth and Bethany pulled up with the stroller, Jackson's excitement was palpable. "Thank you, Baby Jesus," he whispered, eyes shining with gratitude.

"Can I see her, Daddy?" he asked eagerly.

"Just a few minutes, bud," Seth replied, smiling. "Let me get them settled first."

Once Bethany was comfortably resting in their bedroom, cradling Hazel, Seth beckoned Jackson in. The little boy tiptoed into the room, his eyes wide with wonder. There, in his mother's arms, lay his baby sister, a tiny bundle of joy.

Jackson's heart swelled with love as he gazed at Hazel. Her face was scrunched up and red, with the tiniest fingers Jackson had ever seen.

"Isn't she precious?" Bethany's voice was a mix of joy and exhaustion.

Jackson came closer, awe-struck. "She's like a little angel," he whispered. As they gathered around the newest member of their family, the room seemed to glow with an ethereal light, much like the star outside. It was as if the magic of Christmas had descended upon their home, turning a simple prayer into a miraculous moment of joy and new beginnings.

That Christmas, the family felt a deeper connection than ever before. Their hearts were full, their spirits lifted, and their home blessed with the magic of their new arrival. As they celebrated, the nativity scene in the dining room stood as a silent witness to the miracle they had experienced—a reminder that sometimes, the most heartfelt prayers are answered in the most unexpected ways.

Just for Laughs!

What do you call a snowman who vacations in the tropics? A puddle.

Chapter 11

Christmas at Gate 23

Snowflakes danced outside the vast windows of Indianapolis International Airport, creating a picturesque winter scene. Inside, however, the atmosphere was far from festive. A group of weary travelers sat scattered around Gate 23, their faces reflecting the gloom of delayed flights and disrupted plans.

Among them were Andrew and Kayla, a young couple with matching reindeer sweaters. They were huddled together, Kayla's head resting on Andrew's shoulder. "I can't believe this," Kayla sighed, staring at the 'Flight Delayed' sign. "We were supposed to be at my parents' house by now."

Andrew kissed the top of her head. "We'll get there, Kay. Maybe not tonight, but we'll get there."

Nearby, a middle-aged man in a business suit tapped anxiously on his phone. His name was Raj, and he was trying to video call his wife in London. "No, I'm still here," he spoke softly, frustration evident in his voice. "I'm going to miss Evie's first Christmas."

At a corner seat, Mrs. Wright, an elderly woman with a

kind face, wrapped in a hand-knitted shawl, watched the others. She had seen many Christmases, each with its share of joy and disappointment. She reached into her bag, pulling out a tin of homemade cookies. Slowly, she made her way to the young couple.

"Dear, would you like a cookie?" she offered with a warm smile. "Homemade. They always cheer me up."

Kayla looked up, surprised but grateful. "Thank you, that's so kind of you," she said, accepting a cookie.

Raj overheard and walked over, ending his call. "Is that gingerbread?" he asked, trying to mask his sadness with a small smile.

"Yes, it is. My granddaughter's recipe," Mrs. Wright replied, offering him the tin.

As they shared cookies, their conversations began to flow more naturally. Kayla and Andrew talked about their holiday plans, how they were both musicians and were looking forward to performing some carols for Kayla's family.

Raj shared about his daughter, Evie, born just that year, and how he'd been traveling for work more than he liked. "I just want to be there for her first Christmas, you know?" he said, his voice heavy with emotion.

Mrs. Wright listened intently, nodding. "I understand, dear. Christmas is all about family. I'm actually on my way to meet my brother. Haven't seen him in over 50 years," she shared, her eyes twinkling with a mix of excitement and nervousness.

The group's initial discomfort and frustration slowly gave way to a sense of understanding and companionship. They began to share more — stories from past Christmases, family traditions, and even plans that had been thwarted by the storm.

As the clock struck 6:00 pm in the evening, the airport's PA system crackled to life: "Attention passengers, due to the severe weather conditions, all flights have been canceled for the night. We apologize for the inconvenience and wish you a safe and happy holiday season."

There was a collective sigh. They were officially stranded for Christmas.

Chaos ensued at the airport with many passengers frantically booking hotels. The small group, including Andrew, Kayla, Raj, and Mrs. Wright, remained seated, each scrolling through their phones in a futile search for available hotel rooms on Christmas Eve.

After a fruitless effort, Raj, with a practical tone, suggested they embrace the inevitable and stay overnight at the airport. "If the flight schedule changes, we'll be the first ones to know and get on board," he pointed out. Acknowledging the wisdom in his words, the group agreed unanimously, settling in for the night, prepared for an unexpected airport ordeal.

They looked at each other, realizing a strange sense of camaraderie had formed. They were no longer just strangers at a gate; they were companions in an unexpected Christmas layover.

"Hey, why don't we make the best of it?" Andrew suggested with newfound optimism. "We've got music, stories, and Mrs. Wright's amazing cookies. Let's have our own Christmas celebration, right here."

The group smiled, the warmth of human connection beginning to thaw the cold disappointment of their situation. Together, they settled in for a Christmas Eve none of them had planned but would always remember.

As evening set, the mood at Gate 23 had transformed

remarkably. The once-strangers, now companions in misfortune, gathered closer, their hearts warming to the spirit of Christmas despite the circumstances.

Andrew pulled out a small, travel-sized guitar from his backpack. "Well, we might not have a fireplace, but we've got music," he said with a smile.

Kayla joined in, her voice blending perfectly with Andrew's as they started with a soft rendition of "Silent Night." The gentle melody filled the air, casting a serene spell over the group.

Raj, watching them, felt a pang of homesickness but also a sense of joy. He rummaged through his carry-on and brought out a small box of candy. "I was saving these, but we might as well have them now."

"Oh, that looks lovely!" Mrs. Wright asked, eyeing the pretty packaging.

I was going to give this to my daughter Evie, but I think we may need it more than she will," he said, offering the box to the group.

Mrs. Wright, her eyes twinkling in the dim airport light, took a piece. "How wonderful! What a nice thing to share with us. Reminds me of Christmases during the war. We had little, but we shared whatever we had. It wasn't about the lights or the gifts, but the togetherness that mattered."

The group nodded, each lost in their thoughts for a moment. Kayla then shared about how her family would bake cookies together every Christmas Eve, a tradition she missed this year. "But I guess Mrs. Wright's cookies more than made up for that," she added with a grateful smile towards the elderly woman.

Andrew chimed in, "Yeah, and in my family, we'd always

go caroling around the neighborhood. It's funny how music can make any place feel like home."

As they shared stories and traditions, the atmosphere at Gate 23 began to resemble a family gathering. They laughed over Andrew's tales of off-key caroling adventures, empathized with Raj's struggles of balancing work and family, and listened intently to Mrs. Wright's stories from Christmases long past.

"Christmas is about love and kindness," Mrs. Wright said softly. "It's not where we are or what's under the tree. It's the spirit we share, the compassion we show to one another. Like right now, with all of you, I feel the true spirit of Christmas."

Her words resonated with the group, a reminder of the deeper meaning of the holiday. The disappointment of not being where they intended to be on Christmas was slowly replaced by a sense of gratitude for the unexpected camaraderie they found.

As they continued sharing and laughing, the group huddled together, finding comfort in each other's company. The terminal's overhead lights, the gentle strumming of the guitar, and the shared stories and traditions transformed Gate 23 into a cozy, impromptu Christmas celebration.

They were satisfied, but bone tired from the long day.

After their spontaneous gathering tapered off, the group fashioned makeshift beds using carry-ons and jackets, settling down for the night. The quiet hum of the airport embraced them until they slowly drifted off to sleep.

The first light of Christmas morning filtered through the airport windows, casting a soft glow over the group at Gate 23. They stirred from uncomfortable beds, groggy but heartened by the unexpected camaraderie they had found in each other.

While sharing a simple breakfast of coffee and the remaining snacks, Mrs. Wright looked around at her new friends with a gentle smile. "I may not meet my brother today, but finding each of you has been a gift I didn't expect," she said, her eyes sparkling with unshed tears.

Kayla, moved by Mrs. Wright's words, reached across to hold her hand. "You've given us a gift too, Mrs. Wright. The reminder that joy can be found in the most unexpected places."

Andrew nodded in agreement. "Yeah, this might not be the Christmas any of us planned, but it's one we'll always remember."

Raj, reflecting on the night's events, added, "It's strange how life brings people together. This experience... it's something I'll tell Evie about when she's older. How a group of strangers became friends one Christmas at an airport."

Their reflections were interrupted by the airport's PA system. "Attention passengers, we're pleased to announce that the storm has cleared. Flights will be resuming shortly. Merry Christmas and safe travels."

As they gathered their belongings, there was a sense of reluctance to part ways. The bonds formed in the shared adversity of the night were strong and unexpected.

Kayla looked around the group. "Why don't we exchange contact information? I feel like this shouldn't be the end of our story."

"Absolutely," Raj agreed, pulling out his phone. "Who knows, maybe we can all meet up next Christmas, under better circumstances!"

Andrew began to strum his guitar softly, playing a cheerful tune. "Let's make the most of the time we have left. One more song before we go?"

As Andrew played, the group sang along, their voices filling the terminal with warmth and cheer. Other stranded passengers began to gather around, drawn by the music and the infectious spirit of camaraderie.

In those final moments before they went their separate ways, the group realized something profound. They had come to the airport as strangers, each absorbed in their own lives and troubles. But they were leaving as friends, connected by the shared experience of finding light and joy in the midst of a storm.

As they finally parted, with promises to stay in touch and meet again, they knew that this Christmas would be etched in their memories forever. Not because of where they were or what they missed, but because of the unexpected gift of connection they found at Gate 23.

Mrs. Wright, waving goodbye to her new friends, felt a surge of gratitude. "Merry Christmas, everyone. Thank you for this beautiful gift."

And with that, they went their separate ways, carrying with them the warmth of a Christmas Eve spent not with family, but with friends who had become like family. A reminder that sometimes, the best gifts come in the most unexpected packages.

Chapter 12

Amelia's Dollar

On a frosty Christmas Eve, in a quaint little town in Ohio, the air was filled with the sweet melody of Christmas carols and the jingling of a bell. Mr. Schroeder, the elderly bell ringer, stood faithfully by the donation kettle, his face beaming with a kindness that was as much a part of the town's holiday tradition as the twinkling lights.

Little Amelia, a seven-year-old girl with sparkling eyes and a shy smile, approached hesitantly. Clutched in her tiny, mittened hand was a crumpled dollar bill – her entire allowance. She looked up at Mr. Schroeder with earnest eyes.

"This is for the kettle, sir," she whispered, dropping the bill into the kettle with a soft clink.

Mr. Schroeder knelt down, his eyes brimming with warmth. "That's a very generous gift, Amelia. Thank you."

Amelia bit her lip, then bravely offered, "It's all I have, but I wanted to help. Mommy says Christmas is for giving."

Touched deeply, Mr. Schroeder smiled. "You've just shown the true spirit of Christmas, Amelia."

On Christmas morning, a knock echoed through Amelia's humble home. She opened the door to find Mr. Schroeder with a beautifully wrapped present. "This is from Santa, for a very special girl who taught us all about giving," he said, his eyes twinkling.

Inside the box was a new doll, something Amelia had longed for but knew her family couldn't afford. Tears of joy filled her eyes as she hugged Mr. Schroeder.

"Thank you, Santa," she whispered, believing in the magic of Christmas more than ever.

As Mr. Schroeder walked away, he looked back at the joyful scene in Amelia's living room. He knew the town had come together to make this happen, all inspired by the selfless act of a little girl. In that moment, the true spirit of Christmas – giving, love, and community – shone brighter than any Christmas light.

"When one door closes, another opens."

Alexander Graham Bell

Chapter 13

Snowflakes and Second Chances

T he chill of the winter air was palpable as Tiffany hurriedly bundled her children, Mia and Ethan, into their warm coats. Their breaths formed tiny clouds in the frigid Duluth morning. "Hurry up, we're going to be late!" she called out, her voice a mix of cheerfulness and urgency.

Tiffany was the epitome of a hardworking single mother. Her days were a whirlwind of activity, balancing a demanding job at a local law firm with the endless responsibilities of parenting. Mia, her bright-eyed 8-year-old, was always lost in her books, while Ethan, her energetic 6-year-old, could hardly sit still. They were her world, and she worked tirelessly to give them the life they deserved.

But the holiday season brought a different kind of hustle. Christmas, once a time of joy and wonder, now seemed to weigh heavily on Tiffany's shoulders. The festive lights and decorations around Duluth only reminded her of the emptiness she felt without a partner to share these moments. Yet, she refused to let her personal feelings overshadow the magic of Christmas for Mia and Ethan.

As she drove them to school, Tiffany listened to their excited chatter about the upcoming holiday play. They had been practicing for weeks, and tonight was the big performance. Mia was playing a snowflake, and Ethan, much to his delight, was a reindeer. Tiffany's heart swelled with pride, but it was tinged with a hint of sadness. She remembered how her late husband would have loved to see them on stage. He had always been the more theatrical one.

At work, Tiffany struggled to focus. Her mind kept drifting to the play. She wanted to be there early, to get a good seat, to show Mia and Ethan how much their performance meant to her. But as the day dragged on, with meetings and deadlines piling up, her anxiety grew.

Finally, the clock struck five, and Tiffany rushed out of the office. She picked up the kids, who were now bubbling with excitement, and headed home to quickly get them ready for the evening. As she helped Mia into her snowflake costume and adjusted Ethan's reindeer antlers, she felt a mix of excitement and exhaustion. This was their moment, and she wouldn't miss it for the world.

Driving to the school, Tiffany's thoughts were a whirlwind. She wondered if she was doing enough, if her kids felt the lack of their father as acutely as she did. But as they arrived and she saw the joy in Mia and Ethan's eyes, she pushed those thoughts aside.

Tonight was about them, their joy, and the magic of Christmas.

As they entered the bustling school auditorium, Tiffany's heart was full. Despite the challenges, the long days, and the lonely nights, moments like these made it all worthwhile.

She found a seat near the front, her eyes glistening with unshed tears of pride. This was their Christmas, and it was going to be special, just like she had promised.

As the school auditorium filled with the sound of children's laughter and the rustle of parents finding their seats, Tiffany felt a sense of calm wash over her. She watched as Mia and Ethan joined their classmates backstage, their faces alight with excitement. The holiday play was about to begin.

The lights dimmed, and the play started. Tiffany's eyes were glued to the stage, watching Mia and Ethan perform with such joy and abandon. She felt a surge of pride. In these moments, the weight of her struggles seemed to lift, if only temporarily.

During the intermission, Tiffany stepped out into the hallway for a cup of coffee. That's when she noticed him. Josh was hard to miss – a ruggedly handsome man with a warm smile, manning the refreshments stand. He was wearing a firefighter's button on his sweater, which caught Tiffany's attention. Intrigued, she walked over.

"Hi, I'm Josh," he said with a friendly grin, extending his hand. "I help out with my kid's school events when I can."

"Oh, my kids are in the play, too!"

Tiffany introduced herself, and they struck up a conversation. She learned that Josh was a local firefighter who enjoyed giving back to the community. They talked about Duluth, its scenic beauty, and how the city transformed during the holidays. Josh's love for the town was infectious, and Tiffany found herself smiling genuinely for the first time in a long while.

As they talked, Tiffany felt an unexpected connection. Josh was easy to talk to, and he listened with a kind of attentiveness that made her feel heard. She found herself opening up about the challenges of being a single mom and how the holiday season was both beautiful and difficult for her.

"It's tough, isn't it?" Josh said, "Balancing everything as a single parent."

Tiffany nodded, a bit surprised: "You understand that?"

Josh, smiled wistfully, "I do. I lost my wife a few years back. It changes everything."

"I'm so sorry."

Tiffany's heart ached. She understood his pain, but didn't want to get into any of the tragic details of her life on her kid's special night. She looked towards the auditorium and said softly: "It does change everything. But we keep going, for them."

"We do." Josh looked at her with sad eyes. His strength and vulnerability struck a chord in Tiffany. Here was someone who understood loss and the effort it took to find joy again.

The conversation flowed effortlessly until the announcement signaled the end of the intermission. They exchanged a look, a mix of reluctance and understanding, as they parted ways to return to the auditorium.

As Tiffany settled back into her seat, her mind was still on Josh. There was something about him that was both comforting and exciting. It was a feeling she hadn't experienced in a long time.

The final act of the holiday play was in full swing when the unexpected happened. A fierce snowstorm, which had been brewing silently, unleashed its might upon Duluth. The wind howled, rattling the windows of the school auditorium, and in an instant, the building was plunged into darkness.

A power outage.

Panic began to ripple through the audience, a mix of concerned parents and frightened children. In the pitch-black auditorium, the sound of worried voices filled the air. But amidst the chaos, a calm, authoritative voice rose above the rest. It was Josh.

With the confidence of someone trained to handle emergencies, Josh quickly made his way to the stage. Using his flashlight, he guided the children, including Mia and Ethan, to safety. His presence was reassuring, a beacon of stability in the sudden turmoil.

As the teachers and parents worked to comfort the children, Josh had an idea. He found some candles in the main office and distributed them throughout the auditorium. With the soft glow of candlelight casting a warm ambiance, the atmosphere transformed from one of panic to one of communal support.

Josh then encouraged the children to sing Christmas carols. The pure, innocent voices of the children singing in unison created a magical, serene moment. The fear and anxiety melted away, replaced by a sense of togetherness and peace.

Tiffany, witnessing Josh's bravery and kindness, felt a profound sense of gratitude and admiration. In the candlelit room, as the voices of Mia, Ethan, and their classmates filled the air with festive tunes, she realized the true beauty of the season. It wasn't just about the lights or the gifts; it was about community and shared connections.

The children's carols continued when the power suddenly flickered back to life, bathing the room in a warm, welcoming light. The storm outside seemed to have passed, allowing the show to continue.

After the play, as the parents and children started to

leave, Tiffany found Josh. "You were amazing in there, with the kids."

"Just doing what comes naturally, I guess. Helping others, it helps me too."

Tiffany felt drawn to this kind man, an unexpected connection she couldn't explain.

After speaking about their jobs for a few minutes, Tiffany learned something that took her breath away. Josh revealed that he was one of the firefighters who had responded to the accident involving her late husband years ago. Though her husband had ultimately passed away in the hospital, Josh's efforts had given him a fighting chance, a brief hope.

Tiffany felt as if she'd been punched in the gut. Finding out this detail made the events of that horrible night, long ago, come rushing back to her.

She didn't remember Josh's face, or any of the firemen. But again, everything that night had been a blur. Strangely enough, although they were talking about something she'd rather forget, Tiffany found herself feeling grateful to share this moment with Josh. He understood what she'd been going through these past few years.

Feeling Josh's calm energy, and knowing he, too, had lost someone he loved, made Tiffany feel oddly comforted despite the pain. She and Josh had a lot more in common than she'd realized a few moments ago.

Seeing the curious look on Josh's face made Tiffany realize that he, too, was feeling something much more than a casual encounter.

This revelation brought a deeper connection and a sense of fate to their meeting. It was as if the pieces of a puzzle had fallen into place, linking their pasts and hinting at a possible future together.

One of mutual understanding and respect - and maybe something more.

Tiffany spoke first, hesitantly: "Would you... like to get coffee sometime?"

Josh, with a gentle smile said, "I'd like that."

Tiffany and Josh stood there for a moment, the realization of their shared history settling between them. It was a twist of fate, and a promise of hope...for both of them.

For all of them.

As both families walked out of the school together, Tiffany felt happier than she had in years. With fresh snow underfoot and the clear starry sky above, Tiffany felt the magic of the season envelop them. It was a Christmas gift...of second chances and new beginnings.

Chapter 14

Innocent Wonders

Snowflakes danced in the air, blanketing the small Wisconsin town in a gentle layer of white. Morgan watched from her kitchen window, a mug of hastily made coffee in her hand. The serene beauty of the scene outside belied the chaos of her morning routine. Inside her cozy home, the sound of children's laughter and occasional squabbles filled the air.

Morgan, a single mom in her early thirties, had learned to juggle the demands of life with a grace that hid the effort behind it. Her daughter, Olivia, eight years old, was the dreamer, often lost in her world of books and drawings. Noah, her five-year-old son, was the adventurer, always exploring, questioning, and invariably, making a mess.

As the clock ticked closer to their departure time, the morning calm gave way to a flurry of activity. Breakfast dishes were cleared, school bags were packed, and winter coats were donned. Morgan glanced at the calendar hanging on the fridge, its dates filled with reminders of school events, work deadlines, and holiday preparations. Christmas was less than a week away, and the list of undone tasks seemed to grow longer by the hour.

"Mom, where's my red scarf?" Olivia's voice cut through Morgan's thoughts.

"It's in the closet, where you left it last," Morgan called back, her voice a mix of exasperation and affection.

As they finally stepped out into the cold, Morgan took a deep breath, bracing herself for the day ahead. The world outside their home was a stark contrast to the warmth and love within. It was the rush of December, the mad dash towards Christmas, filled with endless errands and responsibilities. Morgan felt the weight of it all, a constant companion amidst the festive cheer.

Morgan navigated the family's old station wagon through the crowded streets of their town. The usual tranquility of Wisconsin's small communities was replaced by the hustle and bustle of the holiday season. Cars lined the streets, and people hurried along the sidewalks, bundled up against the cold.

In the backseat, Olivia and Noah played a game of 'I spy,' but the novelty soon wore off, replaced by the restlessness that comes from being cooped up too long. Olivia's sighs grew louder, and Noah's feet kicked the back of Morgan's seat rhythmically.

"Mom, are we there yet?" Noah asked for what felt like the hundredth time.

"Soon, honey," Morgan replied, her voice strained with the effort to remain calm. The traffic inched forward, a sluggish snake of brake lights and exhaust.

Morgan's thoughts drifted as she drove. The list of errands ran through her mind like a ticker tape: pick up the Christmas tree, buy gifts for the children's teachers, get groceries for the week, and the list went on. The balance between her job at the local library and her role as a mom left little room for error – or relaxation.

As the car crawled through another intersection, Morgan's patience frayed at the edges. The festive songs playing on the radio seemed to mock her growing anxiety. She glanced in the rearview mirror at Olivia and Noah, their faces a mix of boredom and irritation.

It was in this moment of heightened tension, amidst the chaos of traffic and the pressure of the season, that Morgan spotted the church. A banner out front announced a live nativity scene, and the sight of it sparked an idea.

"Kids, how about we take a little detour?" Morgan suggested, her voice brighter than she felt. "Let's go see the nativity scene at the church. I hear they have real animals this year."

Olivia's face lit up at the mention of animals, and even Noah's frown turned into a curious gaze. Morgan took the next turn, steering away from their planned route, unaware of how this simple decision would alter the course of their day – and their Christmas season.

The church loomed ahead, its steeple piercing the grey winter sky. As Morgan turned into the parking lot, a sense of calm seemed to envelop the car, a stark contrast to the chaotic streets they had just left behind. She parked the car, and they all stepped out, welcomed by a crisp breeze that carried the faint sound of Christmas carols.

The live nativity scene was set up on the church lawn, a modest but loving representation of that holy night in Bethlehem. Volunteers costumed as Mary, Joseph, and the wise men stood in silent reverence around a wooden manger. But what caught the children's attention were the animals: a pair of sheep, a gentle-looking cow, and a small donkey, all real and very much alive.

Olivia and Noah ran ahead, their previous frustrations forgotten, replaced by childlike wonder. Morgan followed at a slower pace, her heart lightening with each step. The simplicity of the scene, the animals' soft breathing, and the actors' serene expressions brought a sense of peace she hadn't felt in weeks.

More church volunteers, dressed as shepherds and angels, greeted them with warm smiles. Soft music played in the background, and the scent of pine and hay mingled in the air. For a moment, Morgan felt transported to another time and place, far away from the rush of modern life.

As she watched her children interact with the animals, Morgan felt a wave of gratitude. This impromptu stop, a brief escape from their busy day, was proving to be a much-needed respite for all of them.

Olivia, with her eyes wide in awe, approached the small donkey. The animal stood calmly, its eyes gentle and welcoming. Olivia reached out her hand tentatively, and the donkey nuzzled it softly, making her giggle.

Morgan watched, a smile spreading across her face. There was something about this interaction that tugged at her heartstrings. Olivia's innocence, her pure joy in this simple moment, was a stark reminder of what truly mattered. It wasn't the gifts, the decorations, or the perfect Christmas dinner; it was these moments of unadulterated joy and wonder.

The donkey's soft bray seemed to echo Olivia's laughter, creating a melody that resonated with the spirit of Christmas. Olivia chatted to the animal as if they were old friends, telling it about her school, her favorite books, and how she was looking forward to Christmas.

Morgan's thoughts drifted to her own childhood, to the Christmases of her past. She remembered her parents' efforts to make each Christmas special, not with extravagant gifts, but with love, traditions, and the magic of the season. They had taught her the importance of kindness, of family, and of finding joy in the simple things.

As she stood there, watching Olivia, Morgan felt a shift within her. The stress and worries that had been weighing her down began to lift, replaced by a sense of warmth and contentment. This was what Christmas was about – love, family, and the innocence of a child's heart.

In that small, unassuming churchyard, amidst the animals and the soft hum of Christmas carols, Morgan found a piece of her childhood. And with it, the true spirit of the season.

As Olivia continued to chat with the donkey, an elderly woman approached, her face creased with the lines of many winters but her eyes sparkling with a youthful glimmer. She wore a shawl wrapped tightly around her, and her smile was as warm as the sun breaking through the clouds.

"What a lovely conversation you're having with our little friend here," she said to Olivia, her voice gentle and melodic.

Olivia looked up, her face brightening even more. "I was just telling him about the Christmas play at school. I'm an angel!"

The woman chuckled softly. "I'm sure you're the most radiant angel they've ever seen."

Morgan watched as Olivia and the woman talked. Their conversation drifted from the nativity to Olivia's school, her favorite Christmas songs, and her hopes for Santa's visit. The woman listened intently, nodding and smiling, her presence a comforting force.

It was then that a memory surfaced in Morgan's mind, unbidden but clear as day. She was a child again, sitting beside her own grandmother, listening to stories of Christmases long past. Her grandmother, much like the woman now speaking with Olivia, had a way of making every story magical, every moment special.

Morgan remembered one Christmas in particular when her grandmother had given her a handmade doll. It wasn't fancy or expensive, but it was made with love, and to Morgan, it had been the best gift in the world. Her grandmother had taught her that the value of a gift wasn't in its price tag, but in the love with which it was given.

Tears pricked Morgan's eyes as the memory held her in its gentle embrace. The values her parents and grandmother had instilled in her – love, kindness, the joy of giving – somehow had been lost in the hustle of everyday life. But here, in this moment, surrounded by the simplicity of the nativity scene and the genuine warmth of a stranger's conversation with her daughter, those values resurfaced.

Morgan felt a shift within her, a lifting of the fog that had clouded her vision. She had been so caught up in the chaos of life, in the pursuit of a 'perfect' Christmas, that she had forgotten the real essence of the season.

Watching Olivia and Noah now, their faces alight with joy and wonder, Morgan realized what she had been missing. It wasn't about the perfect gift or the perfect holiday event; it was about these moments, these simple, beautiful moments of connection and joy.

She thought about the recent weeks, the late nights working after the kids had gone to bed, the rushed mornings, the stress of balancing work and home. She had been there, but not really there, always thinking ahead to the next task, the next deadline.

But now, as she stood in the quiet of the churchyard, the sound of Olivia's laughter mixing with the gentle hum of Christmas carols, Morgan knew she needed to change. She wanted to be present, truly present, in these fleeting moments with her children.

This realization was a gift, more precious than anything wrapped under a tree. It was the gift of perspective, the understanding that the most precious moments were often the simplest ones.

Morgan made a silent promise to herself and her children. This Christmas would be different. It would be about being together, about creating memories, about finding joy in the little things. It would be about rediscovering the magic of Christmas through the eyes of her children, and in doing so, reconnecting with the true spirit of the season.

Christmas Eve arrived with a blanket of fresh snow, turning the small Wisconsin town into a winter wonderland. Morgan's household was abuzz with excitement, the air filled with the scent of baking cookies and the sound of holiday music. Morgan, Olivia, and Noah were busy with last-minute decorations, their home a canvas of reds, greens, and twinkling lights.

As evening fell, they gathered in the living room, the tree lights casting a warm glow around them. Morgan had just settled down with a book for Olivia and a hot cocoa for Noah, when a knock came at the door. Puzzled, as they weren't expecting visitors, Morgan opened the door to find a stranger standing on her doorstep.

The stranger was a woman, her face partly hidden

beneath a scarf, but her eyes were kind and familiar. It took Morgan a moment to place her — it was the elderly woman from the nativity scene at the church.

"I hope I'm not intruding," the woman said, her voice as gentle as Morgan remembered. "I have something for your children. A little Christmas surprise."

She handed Morgan a beautifully wrapped package and a smaller, handcrafted envelope. Before Morgan could say anything, the woman smiled, wished them a merry Christmas, and walked away, disappearing into the snowy night.

Inside, the children's curiosity was piqued. They opened the package to find a hand-knitted scarf for Noah and a small, hand-carved wooden angel for Olivia. The envelope contained a note, written in elegant script. It was a story, a simple tale of kindness and giving, inspired by the nativity scene and the conversations the woman had shared with Olivia.

The surprise visit and the thoughtful gifts filled the room with an air of wonder. The act of kindness from a near-stranger, connected to their chance visit to the nativity scene, touched Morgan's heart deeply. It was a reminder of the goodness that existed in the world, of the connections that can be formed in the most unexpected ways.

That night, as Morgan tucked her children into bed, their faces alight with the joy of the day's surprise, she felt a sense of fulfillment and happiness that went beyond the usual holiday cheer. It was a Christmas Eve they would always remember, a serendipitous end to a day of family, love, and unexpected kindness.

Christmas morning dawned bright and clear, the sun casting a golden light over the snow-covered town. Morgan and her children woke early, the excitement of the day propelling them out of bed. They gathered around the tree, its base now surrounded by gifts.

As they opened their presents, laughing and sharing in each other's joy, Morgan felt a profound sense of peace. The stress and worries of the past weeks seemed distant now, replaced by the warmth of the moment.

But it wasn't just the gifts or the festive atmosphere that made this Christmas special. It was the journey they had taken to get here, the lessons learned, and the memories made. Morgan watched Olivia and Noah, their faces bright with happiness, and knew that this Christmas was about more than just material gifts.

It was about the gift of time spent together, of appreciating each other, and of finding joy in the simplest of things. It was about the magic of the season, seen through the eyes of her children, reminding her of the true spirit of Christmas.

As they sat down for their Christmas meal, Morgan felt grateful for everything they had experienced. The serendipitous events of Christmas Eve, the kindness of a stranger, and the rediscovery of what truly mattered had brought them closer together.

This Christmas, Morgan and her children had found something more precious than any gift under the tree. They had found a renewed appreciation for each other, for the beauty of the world around them, and for the magic that the holiday season could bring.

As the day drew to a close, Morgan knew that this Christmas would be etched in their hearts forever. It was a celebration of love, of family, and of the miraculous wonders that could unfold when they least expected it.

"Look at life with the eyes of a child."

Kathe Kollwitz

Chapter 15

Phoenix Rising

Mandy sat in her girlhood room in Minot, North Dakota, surrounded by memories of a life that felt like a distant dream. She gazed around the unchanged space, her eyes stopping at the faded posters and childhood trophies. It was Christmas Eve, and the world outside her window was blanketed in snow, reflecting the cold she felt inside after her recent divorce.

Her mother, Elaine, knocked gently and entered with a tray of freshly baked cookies. "Thought you might like some, honey," she said, placing the tray on the bed.

Mandy forced a smile. "Thanks, Mom. They look great."

Elaine sat beside her, her eyes filled with concern. "Sweetheart, I know this is hard for you, coming back here after your divorce. But remember, you're not alone. We're here for you."

"I know, Mom. It's just... everything reminds me of... what happened," Mandy whispered, her voice trailing off.

Her father, Gary, popped his head in. "Hey, you two. Don't start the party without me!" He held up a Christmas movie. "Thought we could watch this together, like old times."

Mandy's heart ached with nostalgia and pain. "I'll try, Dad," she replied, not sure if she could bear the reminders of her past happiness.

Later that night, Elaine and Gary sat in the kitchen. Elaine sighed, "Gary, I just feel so bad for Mandy. After her divorce, she's been so lonely."

Gary nodded, "I've been thinking the same. Maybe we should do something special for her. Something to lift her spirits."

Elaine's eyes lit up. "What about a kitten? She always loved cats. It could keep her company."

Gary smiled, "That's a great idea, Elaine. A little furry friend might be just what she needs."

On Christmas morning, Mandy was awakened by the sound of her parents playing holiday songs on the stereo downstairs. She dressed slowly, her heart heavy. As she descended the stairs, she was greeted by the sight of her parents standing next to a large gift, almost as big as a refrigerator, wrapped in bright paper.

"Merry Christmas, Mandy!" her parents exclaimed in unison.

"What's this?" Mandy asked, her curiosity piqued despite her sadness.

"Just a little something to cheer you up," Gary said, winking at Elaine.

Mandy began unwrapping the gift, finding another box inside, and then another. With each layer, her frustration slowly melted into amusement, and her heart lightened. The process of unwrapping seemed endless, each box revealing a slightly smaller one. She laughed, genuinely, for the first time in months. By the time she reached the smallest box, a chaotic mountain of cardboard and wrapping paper surrounded her, a remnant of her parents' elaborate plan.

Finally, she reached a very small box with a key inside. "What's this for?" she asked, puzzled.

"Just go to the garage, dear," Elaine urged, a twinkle in her eye.

In the garage, Mandy found the most adorable kitten she had ever seen. It mewed softly and licked her face as she picked it up. Tears of joy welled in her eyes. "Oh, Mom, Dad... thank you," she whispered, hugging them tightly.

As they returned to the living room, the kitten playfully scampered around. Mandy's laughter filled the house, a sound her parents had missed dearly.

Elaine smiled at Gary. "Best Christmas ever?"

"Absolutely," he agreed, watching Mandy play with her new companion.

Mandy looked up, her eyes shining. "You know, I think this is exactly what I needed. A fresh start. With you and this little guy, I feel like everything's going to be okay."

The kitten, now named Phoenix, became a symbol of Mandy's new beginning. She realized that even in her darkest moments, she was never truly alone. Her parents' love and the unexpected joy brought by Phoenix reminded her that life always had a way of surprising her, often in the most beautiful ways.

That Christmas, Mandy rediscovered the warmth of life, even in the midst of pain. It was a Christmas that none of them would ever forget, filled with laughter, love, and the purring of a tiny kitten that brought them all closer together.

Just for Laughs!

from JackAndKitty.com

What happened to the man who stole an
Advent Calendar? He got 25 days.

Chapter 16

The Great Candy Caper

Snowflakes gently floated down in Lansing, Michigan, as the town geared up for its favorite time of the year. The streets were adorned with twinkling lights, and the air was filled with the joyous sounds of the holiday season.

In a cozy house nestled on the outskirts of town, young Ethan sat on the living room floor, his eyes wide with wonder as he gazed at the advent calendar his parents had just given him.

"Remember, Ethan, one piece of candy each day until Christmas!" his mother, Jessi, reminded him with a warm smile.

Ethan's father, Craig, chuckled. "It's a test of patience, buddy. Can you wait each day for your little surprise?"

Ethan nodded eagerly, his fingers itching to open the tiny doors. "I promise, I'll only open one each day!"

Later that evening, after his parents had tucked him into bed, Ethan's mind raced with excitement. The allure of the chocolate behind those tiny cardboard doors was too much for his seven-year-old heart to bear. Quietly, he tiptoed back downstairs to the advent calendar.

"Just one peek," he whispered to himself. One peek turned into one piece, and before he knew it, every door was opened, and all the chocolate was gone. Ethan's heart sank as he realized what he had done. The joy of the moment had faded, leaving behind a pang of guilt.

The next morning, Ethan woke up early. He knew he had to fix his mistake before his parents found out. He scoured the house, gathering small items — buttons from his mother's sewing kit, paper clips from his father's office, and tiny toys from his own collection. With trembling hands, he filled each compartment of the advent calendar and carefully taped it back together.

His parents were none the wiser as they went about their morning routine. Ethan tried to act normal, but his guilt was like a stone in his stomach.

"Ethan, you look a bit pale. Are you okay?" Jessi asked, concern lacing her voice.

"I'm fine, Mom," Ethan replied, forcing a smile. "Just didn't sleep well."

Craig ruffled Ethan's hair. "Well, let's get this day started. Hey, did you open your advent calendar yet?"

Ethan's heart raced. "Uh, not yet. I'll do it later," he stammered, avoiding his father's gaze.

As the day went on, Ethan couldn't shake off the feeling of guilt. Every glance at the taped-up calendar was a reminder of his impulsive act. He wanted to confess, but the fear of disappointing his parents held him back.

That night, as Ethan lay in bed, he realized that the joy of Christmas wasn't just in the chocolates or gifts. It was in the moments shared with his family, in the spirit of honesty and love. With a heavy heart, he decided he would come clean to his parents the next day, ready to face whatever consequences awaited.

Little did Ethan know, the days leading up to Christmas would bring more surprises and lessons than he could have ever imagined.

December in Lansing, Michigan, was a time of joy and celebration, but for Ethan, this year felt different. The secret of the binged chocolate weighed heavily on him, casting a shadow over his usual holiday cheer.

Jessi watched her son from the kitchen as he listlessly hung ornaments on the Christmas tree. "Ethan, aren't you excited to put up the decorations this year?" she asked gently, trying to gauge his mood.

Ethan forced a smile. "Yeah, Mom, it's great. Just a bit tired, I guess," he replied, avoiding her concerned gaze.

Craig joined them in the living room, his brows furrowed in worry. "Buddy, you've been acting a little off lately. Is everything okay at school?"

Ethan nodded silently, his eyes fixed on the Christmas tree. "Everything's fine, Dad." At that moment, Ethan knew he didn't have the heart to tell his parents that he'd eaten all his candy...at least not yet. Maybe tomorrow he'd feel a little better and could confess.

Ethan's parents knew something was amiss. They shared a look of concern, both sensing their son's distress.

Later that evening, after Ethan had gone to bed, Jessi and Craig sat down with a cup of hot cocoa, discussing their son's unusual behavior.

"I think he's hiding something from us," Jessi said, wrapping her hands around the warm mug.

Craig nodded in agreement. "We need to do something

to lift his spirits. How about we organize a little surprise for him?"

"A surprise?" Jessi's eyes lit up. "That's a wonderful idea! Let's plan a neighborhood Christmas gathering. It'll be a great way to bring everyone together and cheer Ethan up."

They spent the next few days planning the event. Invitations were sent out to friends and family, and the neighbors were thrilled to be part of the festive gathering. Decorations were put up around the house, and a menu of holiday treats was prepared.

The day of the gathering arrived, and their home was filled with laughter and the sweet aroma of baked goods. Ethan was surprised to see so many familiar faces in their home.

"Ethan, look! Everyone's here to celebrate with us," Jessi exclaimed, guiding him through the crowd.

Ethan's eyes widened in amazement as he saw his friends, family, and neighbors mingling and enjoying themselves. The house was alive with the warmth of the holiday spirit.

"Wow, this is for us?" Ethan asked, his spirits lifting slightly amidst the joyous atmosphere.

"It's for everyone, especially you," Craig said, putting an arm around his son. "We wanted to bring a little extra Christmas cheer this year."

Ethan felt a glimmer of happiness, but the weight of his secret still lingered. Little did he know, the biggest surprise of the night was yet to come – a surprise that would change everything and reveal the true magic of the Christmas season.

Ethan moved through the crowd, his heart heavy with the secret he had been carrying. He watched his parents laughing and sharing stories with the neighbors, and his guilt intensified. The joy and love in the room only made his burden feel heavier.

Finally, he couldn't hold it in any longer. Pulling his parents aside, Ethan's voice trembled. "Mom, Dad, I have to tell you something about the advent calendar."

Jessi and Craig looked at him, their expressions filled with concern. "What is it, Ethan?" Jessi asked softly.

Ethan's eyes brimmed with tears. "I ate all the chocolates... the first night. And I filled it with other stuff so you wouldn't find out. I feel so bad."

To Ethan's surprise, his parents didn't react with anger or disappointment. Instead, they exchanged a knowing glance and then burst into laughter.

"Oh, Ethan," Craig said, still chuckling. "We knew something was up when we saw the calendar. But we were impressed by your creativity in trying to fix it."

Jessi hugged him tightly. "We're not upset, sweetheart. The important thing is that you told us the truth. That's what really matters."

Ethan's relief was palpable. He felt a weight lift off his shoulders, and for the first time in weeks, he genuinely smiled.

Just then, the neighbors gathered around, and Mrs. Jensen, from next door, stepped forward with a special gift. "Ethan, we've all noticed how down you've been. So, we put together a little something to cheer you up."

She handed him a beautifully crafted homemade advent calendar. Each door was decorated with care, and behind each one was a heartwarming message or small gift from a neighbor.

Ethan was overwhelmed. "You all did this for me?" he asked, his voice filled with wonder.

"Yes, dear," Mrs. Jensen replied. "We wanted to show you the true spirit of Christmas. It's about kindness, community, and forgiveness."

That night, as Ethan went to bed, he felt embraced by the love of his family and neighbors. His heart was full of gratitude and joy.

The next morning, Lansing awoke to a magical Christmas day. Snow covered the town like a glistening blanket, and the air was crisp and fresh.

Ethan and his family exchanged gifts and shared laughter and stories, basking in the warmth of their home. The homemade advent calendar sat prominently in the living room, a testament to the kindness of their community.

As they sat down for Christmas dinner, Ethan looked around the table at the smiling faces of his family. He realized that the true magic of Christmas wasn't in the chocolates or gifts, but in the love and forgiveness shared among family and friends.

And so, in a small cozy house in Lansing, Michigan, Ethan and his family cherished a Christmas filled with unforgettable memories and the true spirit of the season.

Just for Laughs!

from JackAndKitty.com

Why is Santa afraid of getting stuck in a chimney? He has Claus-trophobia.

Chapter 17

Santa's Suit and Father's Love

Christmas Eve in St. Louis Park, Minnesota, was chillier than usual this year. Brent sat by the fireplace, a cup of hot cocoa in hand. His young son, Landon, was nestled beside him. Outside, snowflakes zipped around like fairies in the night sky, setting a magical scene. Brent's gaze fell upon an old photo on the mantel: a younger version of himself with his brother and parents, smiles wide, Christmas tree twinkling in the background.

Earlier in the month, Landon had been involved in a fight at school with an older kid who'd mocked him for still believing in Santa Claus. The teacher had sent a note, expressing concern for Landon.

Landon, still wanting to be reassured that Santa was, in fact, real asked his father for his opinion. "Daddy, tell me a Christmas story from when you were little... about Santa" Landon's voice pulled Brent back from his reverie.

Brent chuckled softly, "Alright, buddy. But this isn't just any story. It's about the year I learned the *real* truth about Santa Claus."

"What the real truth?" Landon's eyes clouded with worry as Brent began his tale.

Brent knew that hearing about Santa would be inevitable once Landon returned to school, and he wanted to be the first to share a very important lesson he'd learned years ago.

"I was nine, just a bit older than you are now," Brent started, his voice tinged with nostalgia. "One day, while searching for hidden Christmas presents, I found something in my parents' closet that changed everything. It was a Santa Claus costume, worn and frayed at the edges."

Landon gasped, "You mean Santa *wasn't* real?"

Brent nodded, "That's what I thought back then. I was angry, felt cheated. All my friends believed in Santa, but there I was, holding his suit in my hands. In my house. That Christmas felt empty, even though my brother and I got presents."

"But, Daddy, why were you sad if Santa brought presents?" Landon asked, puzzled.

Brent sighed, "I didn't understand it then, Landon. Our family didn't have much money. Yet, every Christmas, there were gifts, a feast, and laughter. I failed to see the love behind it all."

Brent eyes brimmed with tears, the affection of that time in his life seemed fresh again as he shared the story with his son.

Years passed, and the fun of Christmas had completely faded for me... until I was an adult and my mother shared a secret. Something I wish I had known when I was your age.

"Grandma told you a secret?" Landon asked, excited to hear what came next.

Yes. Grandma finally explained the truth about Santa. She told me, "Your father worked double shifts from Thanksgiving to Christmas." Tears were in her eyes when she explained our situation. "Your father grew up without a lot of money. He wanted to make sure you never suffered like he did. So, every single year of your childhood he worked as a mall Santa to make ends meet. He wanted you boys to have everything, to never feel like you were missing out."

Brent's voice trembled as he recounted this to Landon, "That's when I realized, Santa *was* real, and he was in my father. Even if I didn't believe in him at the time, Santa *was* real. His hard work, his sacrifices, that was the true point of it all. He loved me and made sure I had a good life."

Landon nestled closer, his eyes wide with wonder. "So, Santa is real? Grandpa's love is Santa?"

"Yes, exactly!" Brent's eyes shone with unshed tears. "And the best part is, the magic of Santa, the spirit of giving, it's something we can all have. We can all be just like Santa."

As he finished the story, there was a soft knock on the door. Brent opened it to find his elderly father, cheeks red from the cold, holding a small, beautifully wrapped gift.

"Dad!" Brent exclaimed, surprised and overjoyed.

"I thought I'd stop by, deliver a little Christmas magic," his father said, a twinkle in his eye.

Landon rushed to him, "Grandpa, you're like Santa!"

His grandfather chuckled, "In a way, I guess I am."

That night, as Landon drifted to sleep, Brent whispered, "Merry Christmas, buddy. Remember, the magic of Santa lives in our hearts, through the love we give and receive."

"Happiness often sneaks through a door you didn't know you left open."

John Barrymore

Chapter 18

A Shiny Penny

Sean, a young, ambitious executive at an advertising firm, gazed out of his office window at the Chicago skyline. It was almost Christmas. The city was alive with holiday spirit, but inside his heart, there was a growing sense of disconnection from his family. His work had been consuming him, leaving little time for his young children, Abigail and Finn.

That evening, as Sean sat at the dinner table, his mind was elsewhere, lost in a sea of emails and deadlines. Abigail, a bright-eyed six-year-old, tried to catch her father's attention with her latest school drawing, while four-year-old Finn excitedly babbled about his day. Sean managed a distracted nod, his eyes glued to his phone.

"Daddy, you never play with us anymore," Abigail's voice broke through his concentration, tinged with disappointment.

Sean looked up, meeting his daughter's earnest eyes. Guilt washed over him. He remembered his own childhood, filled with warmth and family time during the holidays, something he hadn't been able to give his own kids.

That night, unable to sleep, an idea struck him. A puppy. The thought brought a smile to his face. It was sudden, yes, but maybe, just maybe, it could bring some joy and excitement into their home.

The next day, after work, Sean visited a local animal shelter. He walked past rows of eager faces until he came upon a lively golden retriever puppy. Her fur was reddish, almost the shade of a bright copper penny. The puppy's tail wagged furiously as Sean approached, its eyes shining with unspoken stories and adventures. He knew right away - this was the one.

And her name would be Penny.

Carrying the puppy home under the cloak of the evening, Sean felt a flicker of excitement. He imagined the kids' faces lighting up, the joy, the laughter. It had been too long since their home was filled with such genuine happiness.

As he opened the door, Abigail and Finn ran up to greet him, their usual ritual. But this time, Sean had a surprise. He set the puppy down, and it immediately began to scamper around, exploring its new home.

"What's this, Daddy?" Finn asked, his eyes wide with wonder.

"This, my little man, is Penny. She's our new family member," Sean replied, a genuine smile spreading across his face.

Abigail squealed with delight, "A puppy! For us?"

"Yes, for us," Sean said, feeling a warmth in his heart that had been missing for too long.

The kids immediately took to Penny, playing and laughing as the puppy clumsily chased after them. Sean watched them, a sense of contentment settling in. He realized that bringing Penny home wasn't just about giving his kids a Christmas gift. It was about reigniting the bond they shared as a family, a bond that had been strained by his absence.

As the night grew deeper, and the kids fell asleep on the couch, cuddled up next to Penny, Sean made a promise to himself. He would find a way to balance work and family. This Christmas, and every day after, would be different. Penny was more than just a puppy; she was a new beginning for them all.

The arrival of Penny, the golden retriever puppy, transformed the Patterson household into a whirlwind of energy and excitement. Each morning began with Penny's enthusiastic barks and playful jumps, waking the family much earlier than the alarm clock.

One chilly Saturday morning, as snow gently blanketed the streets of downtown Chicago, Sean found himself in the living room, his laptop perched by his side, watching Abigail and Finn play with Penny. The puppy chased after a red ball, her tail wagging wildly, causing laughter to fill the room.

"Daddy, look! Penny is so funny!" Finn exclaimed, clapping his hands in delight.

Sean chuckled, "She sure is a bundle of energy." Realizing his email inbox could wait a few more hours, Sean had an idea. "Hey, how about we do something special today? Let's decorate our Christmas tree!"

Abigail's eyes sparkled with excitement. "Can Penny help too?"

"Of course!" Sean smiled. "She's part of the family now."

Together, they pulled out boxes of Christmas decorations. Penny, curious about every shiny bauble and glittering light, often found herself tangled in a string of Christmas lights, adding to the fun chaos.

As they decorated, Sean shared stories of his childhood Christmases, of grandpa's tall tales by the fireplace and grandma's secret cookie recipes. He hadn't spoken of these memories in years, and recollecting them now made him feel a connection to his past, and a deeper bond with his kids.

That afternoon, Sean felt an unfamiliar emotion stirring in his gut. He realized for the first time in a long while, he didn't *feel* like going back work just yet. He smiled, feeling a lightness in his heart. His email inbox could wait until tomorrow.

Sean suggested baking cookies, a family tradition he had almost forgotten. The kitchen was soon filled with the aroma of gingerbread and cinnamon, as well as the occasional bark from Penny, ever-eager for a taste.

"Daddy, can we make a cookie for Penny too?" Abigail asked, her hands covered in flour.

"Sure, let's make a special dog-friendly one for her," Sean agreed, his heart warming at the thoughtfulness of his daughter.

Later, they bundled up and headed outside, where the world was a winter wonderland. They built a snowman, had a playful snowball fight, and even tried to make snow angels, with Penny enthusiastically jumping into every snow angel, turning them into abstract art.

That day, as Sean watched his children laugh and play, he realized how much of their lives he had missed. Penny, with her innocent playfulness, had opened his eyes to the simple joys of life - joys that were found in moments like these, not in the endless pursuit of career success.

As late afternoon turned to evening, they sat by the fireplace, sipping egg nog. Sean felt a sense of peace and contentment. Penny lay by their feet, tired from the day's adventures, but still wagging her tail in contentment.

"Dad, this was the best day ever," Finn yawned, snuggling closer to Sean.

Abigail nodded in agreement, her eyes slowly closing. "Thank you for Penny, Daddy. She's the best Christmas present."

Sean hugged his children, feeling suddenly sentimental. "You two are my best presents," he whispered, grateful for this unexpected turn in his life that had brought his family closer.

As the flames flickered in the fireplace, casting a warm glow over the room, Sean smiled. Thanks to a playful puppy named Penny, he knew that this Christmas would be one to remember.

Christmas Eve in the Patterson household was bustling with energy and warmth. The tree lights twinkled, and festive music filled the air. Sean, Abigail, and Finn had spent the day baking cookies and playing with Penny, who seemed to understand that this was no ordinary day.

As the evening approached, Sean prepared to read 'Twas the Night Before Christmas' to the kids, a family tradition from his childhood. But when they called for Penny to join them, there was no response. They searched the living room, the kitchen, the bedrooms – but Penny was nowhere to be found.

"Daddy, where's Penny?" Finn's voice trembled with worry.

"I don't know, buddy, but we'll find her," Sean reassured, trying to mask his own concern.

Grabbing their coats, they stepped out into the snowy streets, calling for Penny. The neighborhood was alive with holiday lights and decorations, but the festive mood couldn't ease their growing anxiety.

As they walked, they met various neighbors who joined in the search. Mrs. White, the elderly lady from next door, came out with a flashlight. "Don't you worry, we'll find that little rascal," she said, her voice full of determination.

They searched the local park, the streets they walked with Penny, and even the places they had visited that week. But there was no sign of the golden retriever.

After over an hour of searching, with heavy hearts, they reached the local community center, which was hosting a Christmas event for less fortunate families. They decided to check inside, hoping against hope.

As they entered, they heard a familiar bark. There, amidst a group of children, was Penny, her tail wagging furiously. The kids were laughing, throwing a ball for her to fetch.

"Penny!" Abigail and Finn shouted in unison, running towards her.

The children explained that Penny had followed them from their street and had been keeping them company. Sean's eyes filled with tears of relief and gratitude. He looked around at the smiling faces, the simple yet heartfelt decorations, and felt something shift inside him.

"Can we stay and help, Daddy?" Abigail asked, her eyes shining with compassion.

Sean nodded, "Of course, we can."

They spent the rest of the evening at the community center. Sean, Abigail, and Finn helped serve food, distribute gifts, and share stories. They laughed, listened to Christmas tunes, and felt a connection with people they had just met. Penny, too, seemed to be in her element, bringing joy to everyone around her.

As they walked back home, under the starry Christmas sky, Sean realized that this was what the holiday season was truly about – not just the gifts and the decorations, but the sense of community, of giving, and of being together.

Back home, they gathered around the fireplace, Penny snuggled up beside them. Sean felt an overwhelming sense of love and belonging. This Christmas had taught him the importance of family, of slowing down, and of cherishing the simple moments.

"Merry Christmas, Penny," Finn whispered, hugging the puppy.

"Merry Christmas, kids," Sean replied, his voice full of emotion. "You've given me the best gift of all – a family that's together, happy, and full of love."

As they drifted off to sleep, the house was filled with a sense of peace and contentment. Penny, at the center of this newfound bond, had indeed brought the magic of the season into their lives.

Chapter 19

Mr. Halston's Dilemma

The early morning sun cast a soft, golden glow over Evergreen Acres, but the light did little to warm the chilled air or the heavy hearts of the Cooper family. As Anthony Cooper trudged through the snow, the crunch under his boots echoed the weight on his shoulders. The rows of firs and spruces, once symbols of joy and prosperity, now stood as somber reminders of the farm's uncertain future.

"Dad, do we have enough trees this year?" asked Noelle, Anthony's teenage daughter, her breath forming little clouds in the cold air.

Anthony forced a smile. "We have plenty, Elle. It's not the trees that are the problem."

Noelle glanced at her dad, seeing the worry in eyes. "Is the bank still...?"

Anthony nodded, his expression growing more somber. "Mr. Halston called. He says we have until the end of the month."

Inside the farmhouse, Jill Cooper, Anthony's wife, was

on the phone, her voice a mix of hope and desperation. "Yes, Mr. Halston, we understand, but this farm is more than just our livelihood. It's a part of the community."

The voice on the other end was firm, yet not unkind. "I sympathize with your situation, Mrs. Cooper, but the bank has its policies. I'm sorry."

As Jill hung up, Anthony walked in, stamping the snow off his boots. "Anything?"

Jill shook her head. "No change. He says his hands are tied."

The kitchen was warm, the scent of freshly baked cookies mingling with the pine from the wreath on the door. It was in contradiction to the cold reality outside.

Anthony wrapped his arms around Jill. "We'll figure something out. We always do."

Jill rested her head on his shoulder. "I just can't imagine Christmas without Evergreen Acres. So many families..."

Anthony looked out the window, where a few early customers were starting to arrive, families with children bundled in scarves and mittens. "Let's give them the best Christmas we can. No matter what happens."

The day passed with the usual flurry of activity. Anthony and Noelle helped families pick their perfect tree, Jill served hot cider and cookies, and laughter filled the air. But beneath the merriment, a shadow lingered.

As the sun set, casting a pink hue over the snow-covered farm, the Coopers gathered in the living room, the glow of the fireplace casting flickering shadows on their faces.

"We could talk to the folks in town," suggested Anthony. "Maybe they can help."

Noelle nodded, her eyes bright with a mix of hope and

determination. "People love Evergreen Acres. They won't let it just disappear."

Jill smiled, her family's spirit lifting her own. "Then let's not give up just yet. This farm has given us so many memories. Maybe it's time we ask it to give us a miracle."

Outside, the lights of the Christmas trees twinkled in the growing darkness, a silent indication of the joy and warmth the Coopers had brought to so many. Inside, the family held on to each other, their resolve strengthening.

The Coopers didn't know what the future held, but they knew they wouldn't face it alone. Evergreen Acres, with all its frosty troubles, was more than just a farm. It was home, and they would fight for it with all the spirit of the season they had come to embody.

The air in Stevens Point was filled with the crispness of winter and the soft melodies of Christmas carols. The town, small and close-knit, had always been a place where people supported each other. And now, more than ever, the community rallied behind the Coopers and Evergreen Acres.

At the town hall, a meeting was in full swing. Anthony stood at the front, his voice steady but filled with emotion. "We appreciate all your support. Every bit helps, but we're still far from what we need to save the farm."

People nodded, their faces a mix of concern and determination. "We'll organize a fundraiser," suggested Mrs. Lee, the local bakery owner. "Bake sale, raffle tickets, whatever it takes."

Noelle chimed in, her youthful energy contagious. "And we can have a Christmas concert! The school choir, the local bands..."

The room buzzed with ideas and plans, proof of the farm's place in the hearts of the townspeople.

Meanwhile, across town, Mr. Halston, the stern-faced banker, stood outside Evergreen Acres. He had come to see for himself the place that had caused so much commotion. As he walked through the rows of trees, memories stirred within him – memories of his own childhood, of picking out a tree with his parents.

He paused, listening to the sound of laughter and music. A group of children on a field trip, bundled up in winter coats, were gathered around a fire pit with their teacher, sipping warm apple cider. He watched, unnoticed, as their faces lit up with the joy of the season.

"Remember last year, when you guys found the biggest tree and your Dad had to cut the top off just to fit it in your house?" one child exclaimed, giggling with their friend.

"Yeah, and, my family came here after grandma got better. She said these trees were so pretty," another added, her eyes sparkling with belief.

Mr. Halston felt something tug at his heart. It had been years since he had allowed himself to feel the magic of Christmas. Business, numbers, practicality – these had been his world. But here, in the glow of the fire and the innocence of the children's stories, he felt a warmth he hadn't known in a long time.

Slowly, he walked back to his car, his mind racing. Could he really go through with the repossession? What did it truly mean to protect the interests of the bank, if it meant destroying something so precious to the community?

That night, Mr. Halston sat alone in his office, the only light coming from his desk lamp. In a rare moment of uncertainty, he sat alone, lost in his thoughts, troubled by the enduring hope he had seen in the faces of the children at Evergreen Acres.

He looked at the pictures sitting on his desk. Photos of his family, including one of his late wife, smiled back at him from the frames. She had loved Christmas, loved the traditions and the joy it brought. What would she say about all this?

The next morning, Mr. Halston made a decision. He called Anthony Cooper. "Mr. Cooper, I'd like to meet you at the farm. There are some things we need to discuss."

Anthony, surprised, agreed. As Mr. Halston hung up the phone, he realized his heart felt lighter than it had in years. He wasn't sure what he was going to do, but for the first time, he was open to the possibilities of what the season could bring.

Christmas Eve at Evergreen Acres was alive with twinkling lights and the sweet scent of pine. The Cooper family, despite their worries, prepared for what they feared might be their last Christmas on the farm. The barn was decked out in festive decorations, a beacon of hope in the snowy landscape.

As the sun began to set, casting a golden hue over the farm, a line of cars made its way down the driveway. The townspeople, responding to Anthony telling them of Mr. Halston's unexpected call for a meeting, and wanting to support the Cooper family, arrived with curious and hopeful expressions.

Anthony, Jill, and Noelle greeted their guests, their hearts heavy with uncertainty. "Thank you all for coming," Anthony said, his voice tinged with emotion. "We're not sure what this is about, but we're grateful for your support."

Mr. Halston stepped forward, his usual stern demeanor softened by the entire communities' show of support. "Thank you, Anthony. I asked you all here because I have an announcement to make."

The crowd huddled closer, their breath visible in the cold air.

"I've been doing a lot of thinking," Mr. Halston began, his voice steady but filled with an uncharacteristic warmth. "This farm, Evergreen Acres, it's more than just a piece of property. It's a part of our community, a place of joy and tradition for so many families."

Anthony and Jill exchanged a glance, a flicker of hope in their eyes.

Mr. Halston continued, "My late wife, Martha, she loved this farm. She believed it was a magical place, especially at Christmas. In her memory, and for the good of our community, I've decided not only to delay the repossession but also to invest in Evergreen Acres. To help it grow and thrive."

A murmur of disbelief and joy rippled through the crowd. Noelle's eyes brimmed with tears as she hugged her parents.

"But that's not all," Mr. Halston added. "I want to work with the Coopers and all of you to make this farm a shining example of Christmas spirit, not just for Stevens Point, but for the whole region."

The crowd erupted in cheers and applause. People hugged, some wiping away tears of relief and happiness.

Jill, overcome with emotion, approached Mr. Halston. "Thank you," she said, her voice choked with gratitude. "You've given us the best Christmas gift we could ever ask for."

Mr. Halston smiled, a true, heartfelt smile. "No, thank you. You've reminded me of the true spirit of Christmas. It's about community, joy, and yes, a little bit of magic."

As night fell, the farm came alive with laughter and music. The townspeople gathered around a giant Christmas tree, singing carols and sharing stories. The children played in the snow, their laughter mingling with the jingle of bells.

The Coopers stood together, their arms around each other, looking out at the joyful scene. The miracle of Evergreen Acres had come true, not just in the saving of the farm but in the warmth and unity it had brought to everyone there.

And as the snow began to fall gently, blanketing the world in white, it felt as if the magic of the season had touched every heart. Evergreen Acres, once on the brink of being lost, now glowed with the promise of many more Christmases to come, filled with love, laughter, and the enduring spirit of community.

"A very little key will open a very heavy door."

Charles Dickens

Chapter 20

A Patchwork Quilt

In the heart of Ely, Minnesota, in a small, cozy cottage, lived the Iversons – a family known for their warmth and community spirit. The cottage was adorned with handmade decorations, but the most cherished of all was an old patchwork quilt. Each patch was a memory, a story, sewn with love by Grandma Iverson, who had passed away the previous winter.

As Christmas approached, the Iversons faced a harsh winter. With Mr. Iverson losing his job, they couldn't afford to buy gifts or even a Christmas tree. The mood in the house was somber, but Mrs. Iverson tried to keep spirits high.

"Remember, Christmas isn't about what's under the tree but who's around it," she said one evening, wrapping the quilt around her two children, Lucy and Owen.

"But Mom, it won't feel like Christmas without presents," Lucy sighed, her eyes downcast.

Mrs. Iverson smiled, holding the quilt closer. "Let's share stories about each patch on the quilt. This one," she pointed to a bright red square, "was from your father's first Christmas sweater."

As the family shared memories each day, the quilt seemed to weave its magic, bringing them closer.

One day, Lucy and Owen, wrapped in the patchwork quilt, sat in their snow-dusted backyard, gazing at the sky.

"Owen, do you think Santa will find us this year, even without a tree?" Lucy's voice trembled slightly, her breath forming little clouds in the chilly air.

Owen, trying to be brave for his sister, wrapped the quilt tighter around them. "I think Santa knows where all the good kids live. But I wish we could have given Mom and Dad a real Christmas. They seem so sad."

Lucy nodded, her eyes misty. "Yeah, I heard Mom crying last night. She thinks we were asleep. I just wish we could do something to make them happy."

Unseen by the children, Mrs. Lind, their neighbor, stood by their shared fence, a hand over her heart, listening to the innocent conversation. A wave of compassion washed over her, and a spark of an idea began to form.

"Those kids," she whispered to herself, "they deserve a Christmas miracle. And maybe, just maybe, we can all come together to give them one."

On Christmas Eve, the Iversons woke up to a knock. Outside stood their neighbors, each holding a dish, and a small gift. One neighbor had even cut down a small pine tree for the family. The heartwarming scene left the Iversons speechless.

"We heard you might need a little Christmas spirit," Mrs. Lind said, her eyes twinkling.

The Iversons welcomed their neighbors in, and the cottage was filled with laughter, stories, and the aroma of a shared feast. As the evening grew late, Mrs. Lind handed Mrs. Iverson a small, wrapped box.

Inside was a patch, beautifully embroidered with the words, "Love Thy Neighbor." Tears filled Mrs. Iverson's eyes. She knew this patch needed to be added to their family's quilt.

"Every patch tells a story, and this," she said, her voice filled with emotion, "is the story of how our neighbors saved Christmas."

And so, the patchwork quilt, an old hand-me-down, became woven into the hearts and shared history of the neighborhood – a tapestry not just of fabric, but of love and cherished memories.

Chapter 21

How the Secret Santa Stole My Heart

In the bustling heart of Milwaukee, as the city embraced the festive spirit of Christmas, the Harper & Greene Design Co. office was a small world of its own, filled with the warmth of holiday cheer and the excitement of the season.

Becca, with her bright, engaging smile and an eye for design that could turn the mundane into the extraordinary, was a graphic designer at Harper & Greene. Though she was surrounded by a team of vibrant personalities, she had seldom spoken more than a few words with Aaron, the office's shy yet brilliant IT specialist. Aaron, known for his unassuming presence, often found himself in the quiet corners of the office, solving tech puzzles with a focused determination.

As December's chill brought a sense of anticipation, the office organized its annual Secret Santa gift exchange. This tradition, a highlight of the year, brought a unique thrill to Becca, who loved the mystery and thoughtfulness that came with it.

Little did she know, this year would hold, not one, but a series of little gifts for Becca. All given to her by a mysterious admirer. And it seemed each gift delved deep into her heart, echoing her love for vintage art, classic literature, and the subtle beauty of nature.

The gifts started arriving early, each morning as she arrived at her desk.

The first one was a beautifully illustrated copy of her favorite novel, 'Pride and Prejudice.' It came with a note that read, "To Becca, may the timeless words of Austen fill your holiday season with joy." The handwriting was neat, masculine, and unfamiliar. Her heart fluttered with curiosity. "Who could know me so well?" she wondered, her gaze drifting across the office, searching for a clue in the sea of familiar faces.

Aaron, from his quiet corner, watched Becca with a sense of satisfaction. Choosing these gifts had been a labor of love, an expression of admiration he had long kept hidden. The novel was only the first of the thoughtful gifts he had planned. He'd arranged to be Becca's Secret Santa with his boss, who thought the idea was hopelessly romantic.

"Good luck, Aaron!" Mrs. Greene thought to herself, as she sneakily omitted their names until the very end of the drawing, before slipping them in the envelope as Mike and Becca drew each other's names.

The daily gifts were something Becca was beginning to look forward to every morning. It wasn't *what* her Secret Santa had gotten her, it was the sentiment behind them. She felt she was reading lines from the mystery man's very soul as she read his notes.

Although Becca didn't know who her Secret Santa was, she felt she *knew* him.

Intrigued and determined to uncover the mystery, Becca began leaving notes on her desk, small tokens of gratitude meant for her Secret Santa. "Thank you for the beautiful book. Your thoughtfulness has brightened my day," she wrote, her heart skipping a beat at the thought of this secret exchange.

To her delight, her Secret Santa began responding. The next gift, a set of vintage art postcards, came with a note. "Dear Becca, I'm glad to bring a little joy to your day. May these artworks inspire your beautiful designs." The exchange of notes became their silent conversation, a dance of words that brought a new light to her days.

As the office buzzed with holiday preparations, Becca found herself paying more attention to her colleagues, particularly Aaron, whose shy glances she had started to notice. "Could it be him?" she pondered one evening, as she admired the postcards.

One day, while discussing the Secret Santa gifts with her colleague Jenna, Becca couldn't help but share her excitement. "I don't know who he is, but his gifts are just perfect. It's like he truly understands me," she said, her eyes sparkling with the magic of the season.

Jenna laughed, "Sounds like you have a Christmas admirer, Becca! Maybe this holiday will bring you more than just gifts."

Becca's heart danced at the thought. The Secret Santa exchange was no longer just about the gifts; it was about the connection, the understanding, and the mysterious thrill of an unseen bond. As she placed another note on her desk, thanking her Secret Santa for the latest gift, a charming little succulent, she couldn't help but wonder if this Christmas would reveal more than just the identity of her thoughtful admirer.

As December winds whirled through Milwaukee, dusting the city in sparkling snow, the Harper & Greene Design Co. office was a hive of festive excitement. The annual Christmas party was just around the corner, and with it, the highly anticipated Secret Santa reveal. The office was abuzz with guesses and hushed whispers, but none were more curious and excited than Becca.

In the days leading up to the party, Becca found herself in a series of brief yet meaningful encounters with Aaron. One such instance was during a chance meeting at the office coffee machine.

"Good morning, Becca," Aaron said, a little more confidently than usual, his hands slightly trembling as he held his coffee mug.

"Morning, Aaron!" Becca replied, her eyes lighting up. "Excited for the Christmas party?"

"Yes, quite," Aaron answered, his voice betraying a hint of nervousness. "Are you looking forward to the Secret Santa reveal?"

Becca smiled, her thoughts drifting to the thoughtful gifts and notes. "Definitely! It's been the highlight of my December. I'm really curious to meet my Secret Santa." She paused, looking at him. "What about you?"

Aaron chuckled softly, "Well, I think it's going to be an interesting evening."

Their conversation, brief as it was, left Becca wondering. There was something about Aaron's demeanor, a gentle kindness that resonated with her.

As the party day arrived, the office transformed into a festive wonderland, with shimmering lights, a grand

Christmas tree, and tables laden with holiday treats. Becca, dressed elegantly in a red dress, felt her heart flutter with excitement and a touch of nervousness.

Aaron, on the other hand, felt a whirlwind of emotions. He realized he had fallen for Becca over the course of the past few months, and he was anxious over her reaction. Would she be disappointed to discover he was her Secret Santa? The thought of Becca rejecting him made Aaron's stomach tie up in knots.

Their secret exchanges were the highlight of his day. Aaron often found himself thinking about cute little things she'd said in her notes as he fell asleep at night. Although he hated to admit it, he was a little scared to have his secret revealed to Becca.

The moment of the Secret Santa reveal finally arrived. One by one, colleagues exchanged gifts and laughter, until it was Becca's turn. The anticipation in her eyes was evident as she unwrapped the final gift, a beautifully framed illustration of a scene from 'Pride and Prejudice,' her favorite novel.

"And the Secret Santa for this lovely gift is... Aaron," announced Mrs. Greene, with a beaming smile.

Becca's eyes widened in pleasant surprise as she turned to look at Aaron, who was already walking towards her with a mix of hesitation and hope in his eyes.

"Aaron, it was you all along?" Becca asked, her voice a mixture of surprise and delight.

"Yes, it was me," Aaron confessed, his voice steady but his eyes revealing his vulnerability. "I hope you liked the gifts."

"I loved them," Becca said, her smile genuine and warm. "They were so thoughtful, so... you."

As the party continued around them, they found themselves engrossed in conversation. Although they were surrounded by people, it was as if no one else was in the room. Micheal and Becca spoke of their shared love for classic literature, their fascination with art, and their dreams for the future.

The connection that had begun with anonymous notes and thoughtful gifts deepened into a genuine bond. Aaron and Becca discovered that they shared more than just similar interests; they shared a way of seeing the world, a sense of wonder and appreciation for the little things in life.

As the party drew to a close, and Becca and Aaron found themselves standing by the window, lost in their thoughts.

"You know, this Christmas has been full of surprises," Becca said, her eyes reflecting the twinkling lights.

"Yes, it has," Aaron agreed, his heart full. "And I think the best one was getting to know you."

As they stood there, amidst the laughter and festive music, a gentle peace settled over them. The magic of the Christmas season had brought them together, revealing a special bond that promised the start of something new and beautiful.

The Harper & Greene Christmas party wound down, just as a heavy snowstorm began to sweep over Milwaukee. The city, already adorned in festive lights and decorations, transformed into an enchanting winter wonderland. The snowflakes, each a unique crystal masterpiece, danced through the air, blanketing the streets in a serene layer of white.

Becca stood by the office window, mesmerized by the snow's gentle beauty. Aaron joined her, both of them watching in awe as the city they thought they knew revealed itself in a new, magical light.

"Have you ever seen anything so peaceful?" Becca asked, her eyes reflecting the snow's soft glow.

"It's beautiful," Aaron replied, his gaze not just on the snow but also on Becca, who looked radiant in the enchanting light. "Would you... would you like to take a walk? I mean, in the snow?"

Becca's face lit up with a smile. "I'd love to," she said, excitement tinged in her voice.

Bundled up in their coats and scarves, they stepped out into the snowy night, leaving the warmth of the office behind. The snow muffled the city sounds, creating a tranquil, almost otherworldly atmosphere. As they walked, the fresh snow crunched under their feet, the only sound in the silent night.

They strolled through the snow-covered streets, marveling at the way the holiday lights shimmered through the gentle snowfall. The world around them felt untouched, pure, and full of possibilities.

As they walked, Becca and Aaron shared stories of their childhoods, their dreams, and their love for the Christmas season. Becca spoke of her family's holiday traditions, of baking cookies and singing carols. Aaron shared his love for Christmas stories, especially those that spoke of miracles and the magic of the season.

"It's nights like these that make me believe in the magic of Christmas," Becca said, her breath forming little clouds in the frosty air.

"I couldn't agree more," Aaron replied, his heart swelling with the joy of the moment and the company he was in.

Their path eventually led them to the city's central square, where a towering Christmas tree stood, its lights glowing warmly against the dark sky. A group of carolers, wrapped in colorful scarves and hats, sang classic Christmas tunes beside the tree.

Aaron and Becca stopped to listen, drawn in by the harmonious melodies. As the carolers sang 'Silent Night,' a profound sense of peace enveloped them. The world seemed to stand still, leaving just the two of them under the soft glow of the Christmas lights.

Becca turned to Aaron, her eyes shining with unspoken words. Aaron looked back, his heart beating a nervous but hopeful rhythm. Without a word, they both leaned in, sharing a gentle, tender first kiss beside the Christmas tree, under the watchful eye of the softly falling snow.

As they pulled away, their eyes met, speaking volumes of the feelings that had blossomed between them. Hand in hand, they stood there for a moment longer, letting the magic of the evening wash over them.

"This Christmas," Becca whispered, "brought me the most unexpected, perfect gift."

Aaron squeezed her hand, a smile spreading across his face. "It brought me the same."

As they continued their walk through the winter wonderland, their hearts were full, knowing that this Christmas had indeed brought them the greatest gift of all — each other.

Just for Laughs!

from JackAndKitty.com

How is Christmas exactly like your job?
You do all the work and some fat guy in
a suit gets all the credit.

Chapter 22

Blizzard Bound

The snowflakes danced in the chilly winter air, descending gently upon the small, picturesque village of Winton, Minnesota. It was the kind of place where everyone knew each other's names and stories, a community tightly knit with the warmth of shared memories and experiences. But as Christmas Eve approached, so did an unexpected guest: a fierce blizzard, swirling its way towards Winton, threatening to engulf the village in a blanket of white.

Kodiak, a sturdy husky with a coat as grey as the winter sky, watched the snowfall with a mix of excitement and apprehension. He was more than just a pet; he was the leader of a sled team, and the villagers often relied on him and his musher, Payton, for help during tough times. The team, a group of strong, loyal dogs, shared Kodiak's sense of duty. Each member was an expert in navigating the snowy terrain, their fur coats a spectrum of colors – from pure white to deep brown. And tough times were certainly ahead.

Payton, a young woman with a kind face and eyes that

sparkled with determination, peered out of her cabin window. She knew the storm's arrival meant trouble, especially for the more vulnerable residents. She quickly decided it was time to take action.

"Alright, you guys, we've got work to do," she said, her voice firm yet gentle. Kodiak responded with an eager bark, his tail wagging in anticipation, and his team barked in unison, ready for the challenge.

In the next hour, Payton, worked to prepare the sled. She packed it with essential supplies: food, blankets, and small Christmas gifts that Payton had been collecting for weeks. Despite the howling wind and the ever-intensifying snow, Payton felt a sense of purpose. She dressed warmly, layer upon layer, and then stepped out into the blizzard with Kodiak and the rest of the sled team.

The wind was relentless, and the visibility was near zero. But Kodiak, with his extraordinary sense of direction and unwavering spirit, led the way. The team followed closely, their paws expertly navigating the snow, creating a powerful and rhythmic motion. Payton trusted them implicitly, knowing that the bond they shared was more than just that of a pet and its owner. They were partners, united in their mission to help their community.

As they trudged through the thickening snow, the lights of her cabin faded behind them, swallowed by the whiteout. Payton couldn't help but worry about what lay ahead. The journey was dangerous, and the risks were real. But the thought of the elderly Mr. Swanson, who lived alone at the edge of the village, or the Berg family with their newborn, kept her going.

"Come on, Kodiak! We can do this!" she encouraged the loyal dogs, her voice barely audible over the storm.

Kodiak barked in response, his determination unshaken. Payton was careful to not let her voice show any signs of the worry she felt in her gut.

Sledding through a blizzard is dangerous, even for an experienced team. The temperatures were plummeting by the minute and visibility was next to nothing. It could spell disaster for Payton and her beloved dogs.

Inside her heavy coat, Payton shivered, but her resolve did not waver. Her eyes, squinting against the stinging snow, remained focused on the path ahead. Kodiak, leading the team with a steadfast determination, seemed to understand the gravity of their mission. His paws pushed on, the heavy sled cutting through the snow like a ship through turbulent seas, supported by the strength and resilience of his team.

As they approached the outskirts of Winton, another obstacle presented itself. A large fallen tree, its branches heavy with snow, blocked the narrow path leading into the village. Payton halted the sled, surveying the scene with a mix of frustration and concern. The tree was too big to move and the snow too deep to navigate around it easily.

"We can't turn back now, you guys. We're too close," Payton muttered to herself, her breath forming a cloud of mist in the cold air.

Kodiak, sensing her determination, let out a low, encouraging bark, echoed by his team. He was ready to follow wherever she led.

Payton scanned the area, her eyes landing on a narrower, less familiar path that veered around the obstruction. It was a risk - the path was barely visible, and the snow was deepening by the minute. But time was not on their side, and every moment they delayed meant someone in Winton might be suffering.

"Okay, team, this way!" Payton commanded, her voice firm against the howling wind. She guided the sled onto the new path, relying heavily on Kodiak's instincts, the team's strength, and her knowledge of the area.

The new route was treacherous. Branches laden with snow brushed against them, and the uneven terrain beneath the snow made the journey even more challenging. Kodiak and the team, however, didn't falter. They seemed to understand the importance of their task, moving with a purpose that went beyond simple obedience.

As they navigated through the thick forest, the wind picked up, howling like a wild creature in the night. Payton felt a pang of fear, but she pushed it aside, focusing on the families and individuals who were counting on them.

"Almost there, Kodiak and team. Keep going!" she urged, her voice barely audible over the storm.

As they approached the first house on their route, the silhouette of the small, cozy home emerged through the snowstorm. It was Mrs. Murphy's house, an elderly lady known for her warm smile and the sweet smell of cinnamon cookies that often wafted from her kitchen.

Payton knocked on the door, her heart pounding with anticipation and anxiety. After a few moments, the door creaked open, revealing Mrs. Murphy, her face lighting up with surprise and relief.

"Payton! And Kodiak! How on earth did you make it through this storm?" Mrs. Murphy exclaimed, her voice filled with gratitude.

"We couldn't let you spend Christmas Eve alone, Mrs. Murphy. Here, we brought you some supplies and a little something for the holiday," Payton replied, handing over a package wrapped in festive paper.

Mrs. Murphy's eyes welled up with tears as she accepted the gifts. "You are truly an angel, Payton. And your wonderful dogs are so brave!"

After ensuring Mrs. Murphy was safe and had enough supplies, Payton and her sled dogs continued on their journey. The blizzard seemed to intensify with each passing minute, but so did their resolve.

The next stop was the Berg residence, where a young family with a newborn lived. The path to their home was particularly challenging, with deep snowdrifts that threatened to engulf the sled.

"We've got to push through, team," Payton encouraged, her voice barely audible over the howling wind. "They have a little baby counting on us!" Kodiak, leading the team, seemed to understand the urgency, his steps determined and unwavering.

As they reached the Berg's home, the sight of flickering candlelight through the window brought a sense of relief to Payton's heart. She knocked on the door, and Mr. Berg opened it, his face a mix of surprise and worry.

"Payton, what are you doing out in this storm?" he asked, quickly ushering her inside.

"We're making sure everyone in Winton is safe and has what they need for Christmas. Here, this is for you and your family," Payton said, handing over a package and some essential supplies.

Mr. Berg's gratitude was evident in his voice. "You're a lifesaver, Payton. We were running low on supplies, and with the baby, we were getting worried."

After a brief rest and ensuring the Berg family was well-equipped to weather the storm, Payton and Kodiak resumed their journey. The night was dark, the only light coming from their headlamps and the occasional glimmer of Christmas lights from the houses they passed.

Each stop they made, each grateful face they saw, added to the warmth in their hearts. Despite the cold and the danger, they were bringing hope and cheer to their community, embodying the true spirit of Christmas.

The night was deepening, the sky a canvas of darkness, when Payton, Kodiak and the team made their last delivery. Exhausted but fulfilled, they trudged through the snow, which seemed to be finally relenting. As they made their way back to the heart of Winton, an unexpected calm descended, the fierce winds dying down and the snowflakes gently floating to the ground.

Payton looked up, her weary eyes widening in disbelief. She had never, in her 28 years, experienced anything like this before. Especially after a blizzard. The clouds were parting, revealing a clear, star-studded sky. And there, dancing across the heavens, were the Northern Lights, cascading in waves of green and purple, a celestial ballet of color and light.

"You guys, look!" Payton gasped, her fatigue momentarily forgotten. Kodiak and the other dogs barked joyously, their eyes reflecting the magnificent display above.

The townspeople, alerted by the sudden change, began emerging from their homes, drawn out by the magical sight. One by one, families, couples, and individuals gathered in the town's only intersection, their faces alight with wonder.

Payton and the sled dogs found themselves at the center of this gathering, the community coming together in a spontaneous celebration as they watched the sky. Mr. Swanson, wrapped in a thick coat, approached them, his eyes twinkling with gratitude.

"Payton, you have no idea how much this means to everyone," he said, his voice warm and sincere. "Thanks for helping us out."

The Berg family joined them, their newborn cradled in Mrs. Berg's arms. "We can't believe you risked your life to make sure we were safe. Thank you," she added, her smile bright and heartfelt.

The sentiment was echoed by everyone present. There were handshakes, hugs, and pats on the back. The villagers shared stories of the storm, of the fear and uncertainty they had felt, and how Payton and the sled dogs' arrival had brought not just physical aid but also hope and a sense of community.

Under the glow of the Northern Lights, the people of Winton stood together, the barriers of everyday life melting away like the snow around them. The children played in the thick snow, their laughter ringing through the air.

Everyone gathered together in The Berg's cabin to warm up in front of the fire, while the adults shared hot drinks and late-night Christmas treats.

Payton looked around at the faces of her neighbors and friends. She felt a surge of emotion as she looked at their beloved faces. "Tonight, we're celebrating the fact that we always have each other's backs, through thick and thin," Payton said, her voice clear and strong. "Merry Christmas, everyone!"

As the night drew to a close, the people of Winton dispersed, each returning to their homes with hearts full of joy and gratitude. Payton got Kodiak and the rest of the huskies set up for a nap on the porch, giving them an extra treat for a job well done.

Tired but content, she fell asleep in the warmth of the

Berg's spare bedroom. Payton knew the memories of this extraordinary Christmas would be forever etched in their hearts.

In the silence of the midnight, under the still-dancing lights of the aurora borealis, the village of Winton slept peacefully, united in a newfound appreciation of community and kindness.

Chapter 23

'Twas the Night Before Christmas...in Minnesota

Uff da this poem is as bad as mom's leftover lutefisk sandwich! Seriously though, we hope our friends from Minnesota get a chuckle from our version of the classic Christmas poem.

* * *

'Twas the night before Christmas, in good ol' Minn,
Not a walleye was wiggling, not even a fin;
The stockings were hung by the chimney just right,
In hopes that St. Nick soon would alight;

The children were nestled all snug in their beds,
While dreams of tater tot hotdish danced in their heads;
And Lena in her flannel, and I in my cap,
Had just settled in for a long winter's nap,

When out on the lawn there arose such a clatter,
I sprang from the bed to see what was the matter.

Away to the window I flew like a loon,
Tore open the shutters and searched by the moon.

The moon on the breast of the new-fallen snow
Gave a luster of midday to objects below,
When, what to my wondering eyes should appear,
But a sled full of Grain Belt, and eight burly deer,

With a little old driver, so lively and slick,
I knew in a moment it must be St. Nick.
More rapid than snowmobiles his coursers they came,
And he whooped, and hollered, and called them by name:

"Now, Sven! now, Ole! now, Lars and Torvald!
On, Ingrid! on, Helga! on, Bjorn and Arnald!
To the top of the porch! to the top of the wall!
Now dash away! dash away! dash away all!"

As dry leaves that before the wild blizzard fly,
When they meet with an obstacle, mount to the sky;
So up to the house-top the coursers they flew
With the sled full of goodies, and St. Nick too.

And then, in a twinkling, I heard on the roof
The stomping and pawing of each little hoof.
As I drew in my head, and was turning around,
Down the chimney St. Nick came with a bound.

He was decked out in flannel, from his head to his toe,
With a dash of flour from baking, adding to his glow;
A bundle of hotdish he had tucked in his sack,
And he smelled just like lutefisk — so take a step back!

His eyes—how they twinkled beneath the Northern Lights!
His dimples how jolly, his laugh just delights!
His cheeks were as rosy as a December morn,
With a nose nipped by frost, like when I use the outside back
behind the barn!

The last bit of a jucy lucy he held tight in his mitts,
And the snowflakes, they danced around him in fits;
He had a kind face and a big ol' belly that you'd wanna poke
When he chuckled he sounded like he just heard a bad dad
joke.

He was hearty and warm, a true Minnesotan elf,
And I grinned when I met him, in spite of myself;
With a nod of his head and a soft "Oh, don't cha know,"
No time for a Minnesota goodbye, he had to leave before the
next snow;

So he spoke not a word, and without thinking twice
He filled all the stockings, an example of Minnesota nice.
And laying his finger in front of his nose,
With a cheerful "Uff da," up the chimney he rose!

He sprang to his sled, to his team gave a holler,
And away they all flew, like a fast-flying mallard.
But I heard him exclaim, ere he drove out of sight,
"Happy Christmas to all in Minnesota, uff-da, you betcha!"

Just for Laughs!

from JackAndKitty.com

How did Mary and Joseph know Jesus' weight when he was born? They had a weigh in the manger.

<h1 style="text-align:center">Chapter 24</h1>

Santa Paws and the Missing Cookies

In the cozy town of Winona, Minnesota, the Peterson family welcomed a new member - a playful puppy named Coco. The family was brimming with excitement, especially the two children, Madelyn and Hunter.

Just before Christmas, the family gathered in their warm, festive living room. The Christmas tree twinkled, and the room was decorated with care.

Earlier in the evening, Madelyn and Hunter had been busy baking cookies for Santa. The kitchen was filled with the sweet aroma of their efforts. But as they turned their backs for just a moment, Coco seized his chance and gobbled up the first batch of cookies. "Coco!" they exclaimed, but they couldn't help but laugh at his guilty, yet adorable, face.

Madelyn's face dropped as she realized that there wasn't enough time to bake another batch of cookies for Santa before bedtime. "What are we going to do now?" she pondered, looking to her mom for help.

Just then, as if by a miracle, the doorbell rang.

Mrs. Rice, their neighbor, was standing at their door. "I

got a little carried away with my baking... I guess I made enough for all the neighbors, too!" She laughed, handing them a container of cookies. "For your Christmas Eve," she announced with a smile, before heading next door.

"Thanks so much, Mrs. Rice!" Mrs. Peterson called out, waving to the elderly lady as she continued her deliveries.

"Alright, kids, I guess these cookies are for Santa." Mrs. Peterson said, placing a plate on a high counter. "Let's put these here so Coco can't reach." After perfectly arranging the cookies on the plate for Santa, and adding a glass of milk, the kids decided it was still missing something. They wanted to make it look extra special for Santa. Madelyn and Hunter rummaged through kitchen drawers until they found a red tablecoth. They carefully draped it over the counter, and set the plate of Santas' milk and cookies in the middle, make their offering just right.

"Let's just hope Coco doesn't think these new cookies are for him," laughed Dad, as Coco wagged his tail, unaware of the holiday rules.

As the family drifted to sleep, they heard a loud crash and came running downstairs to find the plate shattered on the floor. Coco, curious and enticed by the scent of cookies in the air, had tugged at the red tablecloth, pulling down the plate of cookies.

"Oh no! Santa's cookies are ruined!" exclaimed Hunter, his face falling.

Mom and Dad exchanged worried glances, wondering how to keep the magic alive.

"It's okay," Mrs. Peterson said, her voice calm. "Maybe Santa doesn't need cookies. Maybe he just needs to know we're happy."

So, the kids wrote a heartfelt note for Santa, explaining the puppy's antics and wishing him a Merry Christmas.

The next morning, the children awoke to a friendly note from Santa, thanking them for their note. Under the tree were special gifts from Santa for Madelyn and Hunter, and even a tiny package of dog toys and biscuits for Coco.

The Petersons laughed about their playful puppy, realizing the mishap with Coco had turned into a moment of understanding. Sometimes, even the biggest messes - this time in the form of a furry bundle of mischief - make the happiest memories.

As the snow covered their house with a soft, white blanket, the children and Coco played with their toys in the living room. The entire family, their hearts full of joy, smiled at each other, grateful for Coco and a very merry Christmas.

Chapter 25

Miracle on Broadway Street

The town of Alexandria, Minnesota, nestled under a pristine blanket of snow, was a postcard of holiday cheer. Twinkling lights hung from every lamppost, and wreaths adorned the doors of the quaint shops lining Broadway Street. The scent of pine and the sound of distant carolers filled the air, creating an atmosphere that could warm even the coldest of hearts.

In the heart of this winter wonderland stood Chelsey's Cafe, a small, cozy establishment that had been a part of Alexandria's landscape for over two decades. Chelsey, the owner, was a fixture in the community. Her warm smile and generous spirit were as much a part of the cafe as the vintage espresso machine that whistled and hummed from morning till night.

But this Christmas was different. Behind her smile, Chelsey carried a heavy heart. The cafe, her life's work and passion, was in jeopardy. The past year had been tough, with rising costs and a drop in visitors. Chelsey had juggled the numbers every which way, but the conclusion was always the same – unless a Christmas miracle happened, she would have to close the cafe doors for good.

Despite this, Chelsey refused to let her spirits be dampened. She was determined to make this Christmas season as magical as ever for her loyal customers. The cafe was more than just a place to get coffee; it was a haven where people came to share stories, laughter, and sometimes, even their sorrows.

The cafe's windows glistened with frosty designs, and inside, the atmosphere was a warm embrace against the chill of the Minnesota winter. Garland and twinkling lights were strung across the ceiling, and a small Christmas tree stood in the corner, decorated with handmade ornaments from customers over the years.

Each morning, as she unlocked the cafe door, Chelsey felt a wave of gratitude for the years of memories contained within these walls. She greeted each customer like an old friend, often knowing their orders by heart. The regulars, a mix of locals and a few who traveled from nearby towns, were the heart of the cafe. They came for Chelsey's special Christmas blend coffee and her famous cinnamon rolls, but stayed for the sense of community that was as much a part of the cafe as its rustic wooden floors.

As Christmas drew nearer, Chelsey found herself reflecting on the journey that had brought her here. She remembered her grandparents, who had first taught her to bake in their own kitchen, filling the air with the scents of gingerbread and sugar cookies. Those were her first lessons in the art of bringing joy through food, lessons she had carried into every cup of coffee and every pastry she served.

Though the future was uncertain, Chelsey was determined to make this holiday season a memorable one. She planned a special Christmas Eve event for the community, wanting to give back to the people who had given her so much. Little did she know, the town of Alexandria was not ready to let go of Chelsey's Cafe. Behind the scenes, a plan was unfolding, one that might just save the cafe and remind Chelsey of the powerful spirit of community and the magic of Christmas.

As the snowy days of December in Alexandria passed, the town buzzed with a secret. Unbeknownst to Chelsey, the heart of this secret was her beloved cafe. Lucas, a local school teacher with a kind spirit and a deep love for the community, had noticed the quiet struggles Chelsey faced. He couldn't bear the thought of the town losing such a cherished gathering spot, a place where he had spent countless afternoons grading papers and enjoying Chelsey's special blend of coffee.

One evening, over cups of steaming hot cocoa at the town's community center, Lucas shared his concerns with a few fellow townspeople. The group quickly realized they all shared the same sentiment. Chelsey's Cafe wasn't just a business; it was a part of their lives, a thread in the fabric of Alexandria. They decided it was time to give back to the woman who had given so much to them.

Lucas spearheaded a secret fundraising campaign, using social media to reach every corner of Alexandria and beyond. He encouraged people to share their favorite memories of the cafe. Soon, the campaign took on a life of its own. Stories poured in from all over – tales of first dates, impromptu family gatherings, and quiet afternoons turned into lifelong friendships, all within the walls of Chelsey's Cafe.

Each story was proof of the cafe's impact on the community. Photos accompanied the posts, showing beaming faces with cups of coffee, laughter around the cozy tables, and Chelsey, always there, smiling and chatting with her customers. The community's response was overwhelming. Donations secretly began to pour in to Lucas, along with messages of hope and support for Chelsey and the cafe.

Meanwhile, Chelsey, blissfully unaware of the community's efforts, was focused on planning the Christmas event at the cafe. She envisioned it as a final thank-you to the community, a chance to create one last beautiful memory in the place she loved so much. She spent her evenings after closing, hanging more decorations, and preparing a special menu for the event. In her heart, Chelsey felt a mix of sadness and gratitude. This could be the last time she would see the cafe filled with the joy and warmth of the holiday season.

As the day of the event drew closer, the town's secret effort continued to grow. Lucas and the other organizers were amazed by the outpouring of support. They knew the time was nearing to reveal their surprise to Chelsey, a moment they all awaited with anticipation and joy.

Chelsey, meanwhile, prepared for the Christmas Eve event with a heavy yet hopeful heart, unaware of the miracle that was unfolding around her. The love and dedication of the community were about to change the course of her story in a way she never could have imagined. The stage was set for a night that would be remembered for years to come, a true testament to the power of community and the magic of the Christmas season in Alexandria.

Christmas Eve in Alexandria was a scene from a snow globe, and at the heart of it all was Chelsey's Cafe. The streets were softly lit with festive lights, and a gentle snow began to fall, blanketing the town in a hush of winter magic. The atmosphere inside the cozy cafe was electric with anticipation. The small space was filled to the brim with decorations, the lights twinkling like stars in a cozy galaxy. The air was rich with the aroma of spiced cider and freshly baked treats.

Chelsey, dressed in her favorite festive apron, welcomed each guest with a warm hug and a brighter smile than they had seen in months. This night, she believed, was her farewell to the cafe that had been her dream for so many years.

She noticed everyone seemed a little more preoccupied than usual, and she wondered if something had happened in the community that she didn't know about.

I guess I have been a little distracted lately, trying to keep the cafe afloat, she thought, a little whisper of sadness tugging at her heart. She felt a little guilty that she hadn't kept up with her beloved customers as much as she usually did.

Chelsey pushed her worries aside and decided to make the most of this farewell party, even if no one else understood it was a goodbye gathering. She put a brave smile on her face and did her best to raise her spirits by as she did what she knew best, serving up treats that warmed peoples hearts and tummies.

She moved through the crowd, serving up slices of her famous Christmas cake and cups of hot cocoa. Though her heart was heavy with the thought that this would be their last Christmas in the cafe, she was determined to make it a night to remember.

The cafe buzzed with laughter and conversation. People shared stories of their favorite moments in the cafe, recalling the many ways Chelsey and her little haven had touched their lives. Amidst the revelry, Chelsey paused to share a quiet moment with Lucas, the school teacher who had become a good friend.

"Lucas, I can't thank you enough for being here tonight," Chelsey said, her voice tinged with emotion. She knew Lucas didn't understand why tonight was so important to her, but it was comforting to have a friend near, even if he wasn't aware tonight was to be the last night of Chelsey's cafe.

"Chelsey, this place has been a second home to so many of us. We couldn't miss this for the world," Lucas replied, his eyes reflecting the room's twinkling lights.

He cast Chelsey a quick glance, his mouth upturned in a mischievous grin.

Before Chelsey could respond, Lucas gestured for attention, silencing the room. "Everyone, if I could have your attention, please," he announced, his voice steady yet full of warmth.

Chelsey looked on, puzzled, as Lucas spoke of the cafe's importance to the community, of how it had become a cornerstone of Alexandria. Then, with a smile, he revealed the secret that had been growing in the hearts of the townspeople: a fundraising campaign to save Chelsey's Cafe.

Tears sprang to Chelsey's eyes as Lucas handed her an envelope. The contents were beyond her wildest dreams – enough to save her beloved cafe. The crowd erupted into cheers and applause, their faces alight with joy and pride.

But the surprises weren't finished. The bell above the cafe door jingled, and in walked a familiar face from Chelsey's past – her childhood friend, Nate, now a successful business owner.

"Nate, what are you doing here?" Chelsey gasped, her surprise evident.

"I heard about the town's secret efforts and knew I had to be a part of this. I've matched the donations, Chelsey. Your cafe is more than a business; it's a heartbeat of this community, and I want to ensure your future here is secure," Nate said, his voice echoing the sentiment of everyone present.

Chelsey, surrounded by her friends, family, and loyal customers, felt a joy unlike any she had ever known. The true spirit of Christmas had revealed itself in the love and support of her community.

As the night came to a close, and the last of the guests departed, Chelsey stood at the window, watching the snowflakes dance in the night. She realized that the greatest gift she had received this Christmas was the reminder that no matter how tough things get, we are never truly alone. In the heart of Alexandria, in a little cafe filled with love, something miraculous had occurred, rekindling the true spirit of the holiday season.

Chelsey smiled and gently closed the cafe curtains. The softness of the fabric beneath her fingertips reminded her of how much she loved this little cafe and the memories its walls held.

Chelsey turned off the lights and sat alone in her joy for a moment, realizing that miracles can happen when hearts truly come together. With an overflowing heart, she peeked out the window one last time before closing up shop for the night. Outside, Alexandria rested under a blanket of snow, serenely drifting off into quiet for the night.

Looking around at her beloved cafe like she was seeing it for the first time, Chelsey chuckled in wonder. She knew, deep in her heart, that a new chapter at Chelsey's cafe was just beginning, born from the love and magic of a Christmas miracle.

Just for Laughs!

I asked my wife what she wanted for Christmas. She told me that nothing would make her happier than a diamond necklace. So I bought her nothing.

Chapter 26

Holiday Cheer

In the glow of festive lights, hearts come to meet,
From snowy plains to city streets, in warmth, they greet.
Diverse voices, laughter mingling in the air,
Celebrating together, a world of care.

Every culture, every soul, sharing holiday cheer,
Songs in different tongues, joyfully clear.
Under the same winter sky, we all gather near,
Uniting in love, spreading hope and holiday cheer.

Chapter 27

Christmas at Heart's Haven

In the heart of a quaint Nebraskan town, blanketed in a layer of pristine snow, the Garcia family home twinkled with festive lights. Chris and Hannah Garcia, along with their children, Mia and Max, had always celebrated Christmas with an unmatched splendor. Their house was the envy of the neighborhood, adorned with glittering decorations and the aroma of freshly baked cookies wafting through the air.

However, this year, as Hannah placed the last ornament on the towering Christmas tree, a sense of emptiness lingered in the air. Chris, noticing the lack of usual cheer, suggested, "Maybe this year, we could try something different for Christmas."

The idea intrigued Hannah, who had also felt the void. "What did you have in mind?" she asked.

Chris, who had recently heard about a local homeless shelter named 'Heart's Haven' needing volunteers for Christmas Eve, shared his thoughts. "How about we spend

Christmas Eve helping out at Heart's Haven? It might be a good way for us all to learn the true spirit of Christmas."

Hannah loved the idea, but Mia, 12, and Max, 9, were less enthusiastic. Accustomed to a Christmas filled with gifts and games, the thought of spending it in a homeless shelter seemed alien to them.

"But what about opening our presents and Grandma's Christmas dinner?" protested Mia.

Max chimed in, "And the Christmas movie marathon we always do?"

Hannah knelt down, her eyes soft but firm. "Christmas is about more than just presents and food. It's about sharing love and kindness, especially with those who need it the most," she explained.

The children, still unsure, nodded hesitantly. The rest of the week passed with the family preparing for their unusual Christmas Eve. Hannah and Chris explained the importance of giving back and being grateful for what they had. They talked about empathy and compassion, trying to instill these values in Mia and Max.

On the night before Christmas Eve, the family sat around the dining table, making handmade cards to give to the people at the shelter. Mia and Max, slowly warming up to the idea, drew pictures and wrote heartfelt messages.

As they went to bed that night, there was a different kind of excitement in the air. It wasn't the anticipation of receiving gifts, but the budding realization of what they were about to give – their time, their love, and a bit of Christmas joy to those who needed it most.

Christmas Eve dawned cold and crisp in the small Nebraska town. The Garcia family, bundled in their warmest coats, scarves, and hats, made their way to 'Heart's

Haven', the local homeless shelter. The shelter, a modest building with a welcoming glow, stood as a beacon of hope amidst the wintry landscape.

Upon their arrival, the Garcias were greeted warmly by the shelter's staff. They were given aprons and assigned to help prepare the Christmas meal. The kitchen was bustling with activity, the air filled with the scents of roasting turkey, baking bread, and simmering vegetables.

Mia and Max, initially hesitant, found themselves in the midst of peeling potatoes and chopping vegetables. It was a new experience, one that took them out of their comfort zone. As they worked, they couldn't help but notice the diverse group of people who had come in from the cold, seeking warmth and a hot meal.

After the meal preparation, the family helped serve the food. It was during this time that they met Mr. Miller, an elderly man with kind eyes and a gentle smile. He sat alone at a corner table, quietly eating his meal. Intrigued, Mia and Max approached him, encouraged by their parents.

Mr. Miller welcomed their company and began to share stories of his past Christmases. He spoke of times filled with laughter, love, and family gatherings – a stark contrast to his current situation. His stories were vivid and heartfelt, painting pictures of happier times, now just memories.

As he spoke, his eyes glistened with unshed tears, not of self-pity, but of gratitude for the memories he cherished. Mia and Max listened, captivated by his tales, their initial discomfort replaced by a deep sense of empathy.

The hours passed, and the family continued to interact with the shelter's guests. They heard stories of hardship and loss, but also of hope and resilience. Each story added a new perspective to their understanding of the true meaning of Christmas.

As the day turned to evening, and the guests began to leave, the Garcias helped clean up. In the quiet aftermath, they gathered in the kitchen to reflect on the day's experiences. As they did the dishes, Hannah and Chris saw a change in their children; the reluctance had transformed into thoughtful contemplation.

"It's not just about the gifts, is it?" Mia said softly, her voice tinged with newfound understanding.

Max nodded, adding, "It's about sharing what we have, even if it's just our time."

Hannah hugged them both, proud of their growth. "Christmas is about giving, not just material things, but giving a part of ourselves to others. Today, you both did just that."

The Garcia family, filled with a sense of contentment, prepared to leave 'Heart's Haven'. Their hearts were full, carrying the weight and warmth of the stories and experiences they had shared.

Just as they were putting on their coats, a commotion at the entrance of the shelter caught their attention. A young woman, her eyes searching and hopeful, stepped inside, her breath visible in the cold air. The shelter staff quickly gathered around her, their expressions turning to ones of quiet excitement.

Mia and Max, curious, tugged at their parents' sleeves, urging them to see what was happening. As the family approached, they recognized Mr. Miller standing up from his table, his face a canvas of disbelief and joy.

The woman was Mr. Miller's estranged daughter, Patricia. She had been searching for her father for months, her journey bringing her to this very shelter. The staff, who had been in touch with her, had been instrumental in orchestrating this reunion.

The room fell silent as Patricia walked towards Mr. Miller. With each step, years of separation and worry melted away. When they finally embraced, it was a scene of profound love and reconciliation. Tears flowed freely, not just from the reunited pair, but from everyone witnessing this magical moment.

Hannah, deeply moved, whispered to Chris, "We should invite them over for Christmas dinner." Chris nodded in agreement, and together they approached the reunited father and daughter.

"Mr. Miller, Patricia, would you like to join our family for Christmas dinner?" Hannah asked, her voice warm with invitation.

Patricia, her eyes still brimming with tears, accepted gratefully, "We would love to."

The Garcias, along with Mr. Miller and Patricia, made their way to the Garcia home. The atmosphere was one of celebration, a festive spirit now magnified by the joy of new friendships and restored relationships.

The dinner table was a vibrant scene of laughter, shared stories, and the clinking of glasses. Mia and Max, who had been so reluctant at first, now basked in the warmth of this expanded sense of family.

As they ate, the conversation flowed effortlessly. Mr. Miller and Patricia shared their story, a tale of miscommunication and lost time, now found and cherished. The evening ended with a toast, led by Chris. "To new beginnings, the joy of giving, and the magic of Christmas," he said, raising his glass.

The room echoed with a chorus of agreement, glasses raised high. The Garcias and their new friends celebrated into the night, united by the unexpected twists of fate that had brought them together.

As the night drew to a close, and the guests departed with hugs and promises to stay in touch, the Garcias sat together, reflecting on the incredible events of the day.

They had begun the day at Hearts Haven believing they were *giving* gifts by volunteering, but by the end, they realized *true gift* was the one they received.

They had discovered the true meaning of the season – a meaning that would stay with them for all their Christmases to come.

from JackAndKitty.com

What do you get when you cross a snowman with a vampire? Frostbite.

Chapter 28

Did Cha Know? 10 Weird Christmas Facts

Explore the secrets behind your favorite Christmas traditions with these weird Christmas facts...

***

1. The Origin of Christmas Trees

Did you know the tradition of the Christmas tree started in 16th-century Germany?

Families would set up trees and decorate them with lighted candles. Imagine the cozy, warm glow!

2. Rockefeller Center's Humble Beginnings

The first Rockefeller Center Christmas tree in 1931 was a small, undecorated tree. Today, it's a grand spectacle with over 50,000 LED lights! Talk about a glow-up!

3. Christmas Movies: Surprising Facts

"It's a Wonderful Life," a holiday favorite, was actually a box-office flop at first. And did you know Tom Hanks played six roles in "The Polar Express"?

4. Elf on the Shelf's Original Name

The Elf on the Shelf tradition started with an elf named Fisbee in the 1970s. This little elf has become a holiday staple in many homes.

5. The Real Title of a Christmas Classic

""Twas the Night Before Christmas" is actually titled "A Visit from St. Nicholas." A single line can change everything!

6. Christmas in Space and Song Records

"Jingle Bells" was the first song played in space, and Bing Crosby's "White Christmas" is the best-selling single ever. Talk about holiday hits!

7. Rudolph's Marketing Origins

Rudolph the Red-Nosed Reindeer first appeared in a 1939 Montgomery Ward coloring book. From marketing to Christmas icon!

8. Mistletoe's Mythical Roots

Kissing under the mistletoe might date back to Norse mythology. This romantic tradition has ancient origins.

9. Christmas: Once Banned, Now Beloved

Christmas wasn't always celebrated. It was even banned in the mid-17th century. Now, it's a global festivity.

10. The Real Busiest Shopping Days

Forget Black Friday; the Friday and Saturday before Christmas are the busiest shopping days. Last-minute gifts, anyone?

* * *

We hope you enjoyed these quirky Christmas facts. There's always something fun to discover about the holidays. Happy exploring and Merry Christmas! - Jack and Kitty

"In a gentle way, you can shake the
world."

Mahatma Gandhi

Chapter 29

Buddy's Christmas Journey

In the cozy town of Bismarck, North Dakota, where winters were long and the snowfall generous, the Anderson family was preparing for their favorite season: Christmas. Their home, a charming, two-story house on Elm Street, was already adorned with twinkling lights and festive decorations. The heart of this warm family was Buddy, a golden retriever with a coat as bright as the sun and a tail that never stopped wagging.

One crisp December morning, with Christmas just a week away, the Andersons decided to continue their annual tradition of choosing a Christmas tree from the nearby forest. Wrapped in scarves and mittens, they piled into the family car, a red SUV, with Buddy excitedly jumping in last. His nose pressed against the window, Buddy watched the familiar streets give way to the white expanse of the forest.

The forest was a winter wonderland, with trees clothed in snow and the air filled with the scent of pine. Buddy, overjoyed by the new sights and smells, darted between the trees, his golden fur a blur against the snow. The Andersons laughed and called after him, their voices echoing through the woods.

As the family ventured deeper into the forest, entranced by the perfect tree, Buddy's curiosity led him farther away. Distracted by a squirrel, he chased it through the thickening woods, oblivious to the distance he was putting between himself and his family.

The squirrel proved too elusive, and soon, Buddy found himself alone, the familiar sounds of his family replaced by the silence of the forest. He wandered, trying to trace his steps back, but everything looked the same under the heavy blanket of snow.

Back at the tree they had chosen, the Andersons suddenly realized Buddy's absence. Panic set in as they called his name, their voices growing more desperate. They split up, each taking a different path, their footprints criss-crossing in the snow.

Hours passed, the sky dimming as the sun began to set. The temperature dropped, and the once welcoming forest grew cold and menacing. Buddy, tired and scared, found shelter under a large pine tree, its branches heavy with snow.

The Andersons, realizing the futility of their search as darkness enveloped the forest, made the heart-wrenching decision to return home. The car ride back was silent, each member lost in worry and guilt. They promised to resume the search at dawn, clinging to the hope that Buddy would find his way back to them.

That night, as they huddled around the fireplace, the Andersons couldn't help but glance at Buddy's empty bed, the absence of their cheerful companion leaving a void in their hearts. Meanwhile, in the cold embrace of the forest, Buddy curled up under the tree, the snow gently falling around him, the silent night bearing witness to his frosty farewell.

As dawn broke over the snowy landscape of Bismarck, Buddy awoke under the pine tree, shivering and hungry. He missed the warmth of his home and the loving touch of the Andersons. With determination, he began to wander again, hoping to find a familiar landmark.

On the outskirts of town, nestled among a grove of trees, stood a small, somewhat weathered house. It belonged to Mr. Gregory Campbell, a widower in his late seventies. Mr. Campbell lived a solitary life, his days marked by the quiet routine of a man who had lost too much. Once a vibrant soul with a family, he now found his home echoing with the memories of a past life.

That morning, as Mr. Campbell sipped his coffee by the window, his eyes caught a glimpse of golden fur moving through the trees. Curiosity piqued, he put on his coat and stepped outside, just in time to see Buddy approach, tentative and tired.

Buddy, sensing kindness in the stranger's eyes, wagged his tail weakly. Mr. Campbell, seeing the dog's condition, immediately felt a surge of compassion. He knelt down, offering his hand for Buddy to sniff, and whispered soothing words. Buddy, driven by instinct and the need for comfort, allowed this gentle stranger to pet him.

Mr. Campbell led Buddy inside, where he prepared a warm spot near the fireplace and fed him. As Buddy ate, Mr. Campbell examined him, noticing the collar and realizing he must belong to someone. Yet, there was something about this golden retriever, a sense of understanding and companionship, that filled a void in Mr. Campbell's heart.

Meanwhile, the Anderson family was spreading the

word about their missing Buddy. Flyers were posted, social media pleas were shared, and the local community joined in the search. Despite their efforts, the days passed with no sign of Buddy. Their home felt emptier, the joy of the holiday season overshadowed by their loss.

Back at Mr. Campbell's house, a routine began to form. Buddy would accompany Mr. Campbell on his short walks, their steps slow but steady, leaving twin trails in the snow. In the evenings, they sat by the fire, Mr. Campbell often speaking to Buddy about his life, retirement and fondest memories. Buddy, for his part, listened, his presence a silent comfort.

As Christmas drew nearer, Mr. Campbell found himself looking forward to each day, something he hadn't felt in years. Buddy, though still missing his own family, found solace in the kindness of this lonely old man. In their own way, they saved each other, filling their days with companionship and a newfound sense of purpose.

Their bond, formed in the heart of a cold winter, spoke of the unexpected friendships that can arise in life's most challenging moments. For Mr. Campbell and Buddy, this Christmas was shaping up to be one unlike any other, filled with the warmth of friendship and the healing power of kindness.

Christmas Eve in Bismarck was a scene straight from a postcard, with homes decorated in festive lights and the air filled with the anticipation of the holiday. In the Anderson household, however, the festive spirit was subdued, the absence of Buddy casting a shadow over the celebrations.

Mr. Campbell and Buddy had settled into a comfortable routine, the old man finding joy in the dog's company. He had even hung a stocking for Buddy, filling it with treats. Yet, he couldn't shake the feeling that Buddy belonged somewhere else, with a family that was surely missing him dearly.

As the day progressed, a miracle was quietly unfolding. A local, recognizing Buddy from the flyers, had spotted him through Mr. Campbell's window. Knowing the Andersons' plight, they quickly informed them.

With a mix of apprehension and hope, the Anderson family, led by the tip, found themselves at Mr. Campbell's doorstep. Mrs. Anderson, holding back tears, rang the bell. Mr. Campbell, surprised by the visitors, opened the door to find a family with eyes brimming with hope and anxiety.

The moment Buddy heard the familiar voices, he bounded to the door, his tail wagging furiously. The reunion was emotional and heartwarming, with tears and laughter filling the room as Buddy licked and jumped on his beloved family. Mr. Campbell, standing back, watched the scene with a bittersweet feeling in his heart.

The Andersons, overwhelmed with gratitude, turned to Mr. Campbell, their expressions conveying a depth of thanks words couldn't express. As they learned of his kindness in taking care of Buddy, they saw the loneliness in his eyes, the same loneliness that had haunted their home in Buddy's absence.

In a moment of heartfelt generosity, Mr. Anderson extended an invitation to Mr. Campbell to join them for Christmas dinner. "It's the least we can do to thank you," he said, "and we'd be honored to have you with us."

Mr. Campbell, taken aback by the gesture, felt a warmth he hadn't experienced in years. Accepting the invitation, he found himself part of a Christmas celebration that was filled with joy, laughter, and stories.

The dinner table that evening was a symbol of newfound

friendships and the spirit of the holiday season bringing people together. The Andersons and Mr. Campbell shared stories, Buddy resting contentedly at their feet, his presence a reminder of the miracle that had brought them all together.

As they exchanged gifts and sang carols, the true magic of Christmas was palpable in the room. Mr. Campbell, looking around at the smiling faces, felt a sense of belonging. For the Andersons, having Buddy back and witnessing the joy he brought to Mr. Campbell was the best Christmas gift they could have asked for.

That night, as they bid Mr. Campbell goodbye, promises were made to stay in touch and bring Buddy to visit often. As the snow continued to fall gently outside, the Anderson family snuggled with their reunited pet, content and happy. The spirit of the season seemed to whisper of hope, love, and the endless possibilities of friendship.

Chapter 30

Homecoming Under the Stars

S nowflakes gently kissed the windowpanes of the Clark family home in Chicago, draping the city in a blanket of white as the holiday season approached. Inside, the warmth of the fireplace and the twinkling lights of the Christmas tree contrasted with the chilly winter outside.

Mandy Clark, with her heart full of mixed emotions, gathered her two children, eight-year-old Sophie and five-year-old Aiden, in the living room. The reason for this family huddle was a special delivery: a care package from their father, Ty, who was serving overseas in the military.

"Do you think Dad remembered to send a present?" Sophie asked curiously as Mandy opened the package. Mandy smiled and replied, "Your dad always remembers, sweetie."

Ty's absence was felt deeply by each member of the Clark family, especially during the festive season. But this package, wrapped in love and care, brought a piece of him home. Mandy's hands trembled slightly as she opened it, revealing an array of gifts and notes, each item meticulously chosen by Ty to convey his love and presence.

For Sophie, there was a book about stars and planets, a shared interest with her dad. It came with a note: "To my little astronomer, look up at the stars and think of our adventures." Sophie clutched the book to her chest, imagining her father under the same starry sky.

Aiden unwrapped a small toy soldier, a replica of what Ty wore. "Look, Mom! It's just like Dad!" Aiden exclaimed with excitement. Mandy responded warmly, "Yes, it is, Aiden." The note attached read, "To my brave little man, always stand tall and strong." Aiden's eyes lit up, proudly holding the figure high.

Mandy's gift was a delicate necklace with a pendant, a locket containing a family photo. The note with it said, "To my love, close to your heart until I'm home." Tears welled up in Mandy's eyes as she felt the weight of the locket, a symbol of their enduring love and the distance between them. She whispered to herself, "We miss you so much, Ty."

Mandy and her children spent the evening reminiscing about their time with Ty before he went overseas, each memory a precious reminder of their love and unity. They all had a good laugh recounting Ty's love of funny pranks, and how much they all loved watching cartoons together as a family.

As the children finally drifted to sleep, Mandy sat by the window, watching the snowfall. She whispered a prayer for Ty's safe return, her eyes reflecting the holiday lights. The care package had not only brought joy and memories but also a renewed sense of hope and strength.

The next day was Christmas Eve and the family missed

Ty's presence more than ever. They decided to distract themselves with an evening walk.

The streets of downtown Chicago were alive with the spirit of Christmas. Twinkling lights adorned every lamppost, and holiday cheer filled the air. The Clark family, despite the void left by Ty's absence, was determined to immerse themselves in the festivities.

Mandy, Sophie, and Aiden, bundled up in their warmest coats, walked hand in hand through the bustling crowds. "I wish Daddy could see these lights with us," Sophie said. Mandy comforted her, "He's with us in spirit, Sophie, and he loves Christmas lights just as much as we do."

They admired the grand holiday displays in store windows and swayed in time to the cheerful Christmas music blaring from the speakers above the business doors. The giant Christmas tree in the city square, decked out in shimmering ornaments and lights, stood as a beacon of the season's joy and wonder.

"Dad would have loved to pick the star for the top of the tree," Aiden commented as they admired the Christmas tree. Mandy agreed, "He sure would have, Aiden."

As they all sipped hot cocoa she'd grabbed from a nearby street vendor, Mandy watched her children's faces light up with excitement, their laughter mingling with the festive sounds around them. She felt a bittersweet pang, wishing Ty could share this moment with them. But she smiled, knowing he would want them to enjoy the holiday despite his absence.

Meanwhile, halfway across the world, Ty had been busy arranging a special surprise for his family - an unexpected journey home. After months of longing and waiting, he had received last-minute leave and was now racing against time to make it home for Christmas. His journey was fraught with challenges – delayed flights, winter storms, and the sheer distance he had to cover.

Each leg of Ty's journey was a battle against the odds. He navigated crowded airports, endured long layovers, and faced the uncertainty of winter travel. Yet, his determination never wavered. The thought of surprising his family, of seeing their faces light up when he walked through the door, fueled his resolve.

Back in Chicago, the Clarks concluded their evening at the community event with a visit to a local church for a Christmas Eve service. The hymns and readings, echoing through the candlelit sanctuary, filled their hearts with peace and hope. Mandy held her children close, her thoughts drifting to Ty, praying for his safety as he served overseas.

The night sky over Chicago was a blanket of twinkling stars, casting a serene glow over the city. The Clark family, their hearts warmed by the day's festivities, walked up the path to their home, their laughter and chatter filling the cold Christmas Eve air.

As they approached their house, Sophie was the first to see the surprise. She gasped, then cried out, running as fast as her little legs could carry her. "Daddy!" she squealed, jumping into his arms.

"Sophie, sweetie!" Ty exclaimed, kissing her forehead and spinning her around, barely able to contain his joy. Aiden soon followed, barreling into his father's arms before he had time to set Sophie down. The three toppled over into the soft snow on the front lawn, laughing hysterically at the mishap.

The sight of her husband, safely home and as handsome as ever, took Mandy's breath away. For a moment, time seemed to stand still, and she felt as if this weren't real, but a dream too impossibly good to be true.

Sophie and Aiden squealed with delight, their small feet crunching in the snow as they made snowballs and chased each other. Mandy, overwhelmed with emotion, walked up to Ty, tears streaming down her face. "I don't understand what's happening. You're supposed to be gone until next year! How did you get here?" she said through her tears.

"It was pretty easy once I boarded. The airplane did all the hard work flying," Ty joked with a smile of amusement.

Mandy laughed, a tear of relief sliding down her cheek.

Ty's voice was tender and soft. "I left the *moment* I found out I could. You and the kids are my world."

Their embrace was a long, heartfelt moment of reunion, filled with love and relief. Ty, looking into the eyes of his wife and beloved family, felt a wave of happiness and gratitude. Even after all those lonely nights - those difficult moments where all he had was their picture, or the fading remnants of their last video call, after all of those times he'd fantasized about this very moment of their reunion - he still couldn't believe it.

He was here.

And Mandy had never looked more beautiful than she did at that moment, staring at him with such admiration and affection. The hardships of his journey melted away under the warmth of her touch. He was home, finally, where he belonged.

The family stood there under the twinkling Christmas lights, their joyous laughter echoing in the night. Neighbors peeked out of their windows, smiling at the heartwarming scene. The Clark family, reunited at last, was a living embodiment of hope

Once inside, they gathered around the fireplace, sharing stories and opening the gifts that Ty had brought. "So, how did you two like the gifts I sent?" Ty asked. Sophie and Aiden excitedly shared their stories about the gifts, filling the room with laughter and warmth. Each present was a token of his love, chosen during his time away. The children showed him the gifts he had sent earlier, their eyes shining with excitement.

Ty and Mandy, with their children nestled close, reflected on the true meaning of Christmas. It wasn't just about the gifts or the decorations; it was about love, family, and the miracles that can happen when you least expect them.

As they settled into their familiar Christmas Eve routine of previous years, the house filled with the scents of hot chocolate and freshly baked cookies. Outside, the stars continued to shine, a silent witness to the magic and love that had unfolded below.

It would be a Christmas they would always remember, even after Ty returned to his station a few weeks later. That holiday was a time of joy, of unexpected reunions, and a powerful bond that held them together through thick and thin. In their hearts, they knew this was the true spirit of the season: the enduring power of love for your family - regardless of how many miles, or circumstances that may separate you.

How do you wash your hands over the holiday? With Santatizer.

Chapter 31

The Miracle in the Snow

In the heart of Minneapolis, the Johnson family's home buzzed with the warmth and cheer of Christmas preparations. The scent of cinnamon and pine filled the air, and festive tunes played softly in the background. Emily Johnson meticulously adorned the Christmas tree with twinkling lights and heirloom ornaments, while her two children, Lily and Max, eagerly helped, their faces lit up with excitement.

Tom, Emily's husband, was in the kitchen, perfecting his famous gingerbread cookie recipe. Their dog, Luna, wagged her tail, eagerly waiting for any crumbs that might fall her way. Despite the joy and hustle of the season, there was a noticeable emptiness in Emily's heart. She missed her parents, who lived in the small, picturesque town of Harmony, about three hours away from Minneapolis.

Every year, the family tradition was to spend Christmas at her parents' home, but this year, the weather forecast warned of a massive snowstorm hitting Minnesota. Emily had almost resigned herself to the idea of a Christmas without her parents when Tom, ever the optimist, suggested they try to make the journey before the storm hit its peak. "It might be our only chance to be together for Christmas," he said, his voice filled with hope.

After a family huddle, they decided to embark on the journey, packed with warm clothes, presents, and an array of Christmas treats. They wanted to surprise Grandma and Grandpa, bringing the Christmas spirit right to their doorstep. With the car loaded and the family bundled up, they set off under a sky heavy with snow-laden clouds, hopeful and determined to make it to Harmony in time for a late lunch on Christmas Eve.

The journey began with laughter and singing along to Christmas carols. Snowflakes began to fall gently, dusting the landscape in a delicate layer of white. The beauty of Minnesota's winter was on full display, with pine trees lining the road, standing tall and proud under their snowy mantles.

But as they traveled further, the gentle snowfall transformed into a fierce blizzard. The wind howled, and the snow swirled around the car, reducing visibility to nearly zero. Tom gripped the steering wheel tightly, his knuckles white, as he strained to see the road ahead. Emily kept a brave face for the kids, but her heart raced with worry.

"Are we going to be okay, Mommy?" Lily's small voice broke the tense silence.

"Yes, sweetheart, your dad's a great driver. We'll be okay," Emily reassured her, though her own confidence wavered.

The once familiar route became unrecognizable, hidden under a blanket of snow. They missed a crucial turn and found themselves on an unfamiliar, desolate road. The car's headlights barely penetrated the thick curtain of snow. After struggling through the wet, heavy snow, the car finally got stuck, its wheels spinning uselessly in a snowdrift.

Emily tried to use her cell to call for help, but had no service in the remote location. It was getting dim outside, and she didn't know how long the gas in the tank would last to keep the car running and warm. She knew she needed to stay calm for her kids, but she was worried about their safety.

She tried not to panic and, instead, gave Tom's hand a little squeeze of encouragement.

He gave her a little smile, trying to remain optimistic, but Emily could see concern crease her husband's forehead.

Stranded and miles away from Harmony, the warmth of the car was their only solace in the midst of the howling wilderness. The family huddled together, trying to stay calm, watching as the snowflakes danced wildly in the beam of the headlights. The magical winter wonderland they had admired just hours ago now seemed like a frozen labyrinth, holding them in its icy grasp.

Even their dog Luna seemed to sense their concern. She huddled between the children, resting her head on Lily's lap.

As the reality of their situation set in, they clung to each other, a beacon of love and hope in the midst of the storm. Unbeknownst to them, their Christmas miracle was just around the corner, ready to emerge from the heart of the Minnesota blizzard.

As the Johnson family sat anxious in their stranded car, the blizzard raging outside, hope seemed to be fading with each passing minute. Suddenly, through the thick curtain of snow, a figure emerged, approaching their car. He was a robust man, with a thick beard and a friendly smile that seemed to light up the gloomy surroundings. His eyes twinkled with a kindness that immediately put the family at ease.

"I'm Nick, a woodsman from around these parts," he introduced himself, his voice booming yet warm. "You folks look like you could use some help."

Relief washed over the family as they eagerly accepted his offer of shelter. Nick led them through the snowy landscape to a quaint cabin, hidden away in the woods. It was as if they had stepped into a storybook, with the cabin's warm glow providing a stark contrast to the cold, white world outside.

As they entered the cabin, they were enveloped by a warmth that went beyond the crackling fireplace. There was something magical about the place, with its cozy decor and the faint scent of pine and cinnamon in the air. Nick's demeanor was jolly and welcoming, and there was an air of mystery about him that intrigued the family.

Inside Nick's cabin, the atmosphere was one of instant festive cheer. The cabin was adorned with handmade Christmas decorations, and a small, beautifully decorated tree stood in the corner. Nick busied himself in the kitchen, preparing hot cocoa and a hearty meal, humming Christmas tunes as he worked.

The family settled in, their earlier apprehension replaced by a sense of wonder. Luna sniffed around, finding new scents throughout the cozy cabin, before finally settling down on the couch for a nap. She liked it here.

As they all sipped on the rich cocoa and ate a delicious meal, Nick shared stories of his life in the woods, each tale more fascinating than the last. His stories were filled with a sense of wonder and magic, captivating the children and adults alike.

After dinner, they gathered around the fireplace. Nick brought out an old guitar and began playing carols. The family joined in, singing along, their voices filling the cabin with joy and laughter. It was a spontaneous Christmas celebration, one that none of them had expected but all deeply cherished.

As the evening wore on, the magic of the cabin and Nick's presence seemed to grow. Small, unexplainable occurrences – like the way the shadows danced merrily around the room or the faintest hint of jingling of bells whenever Nick moved – added to the enchanting experience. It was as if they had been transported to a realm where the worries of the world didn't exist, where the spirit of Christmas was alive and tangible.

In that enchanted cabin, with a stranger who felt like an old friend, the Johnson family found a joy and peace they hadn't known they were missing. Nick gave the family his bedroom for the night, and moved out onto the living room sofa. An extra heap of warm blankets and pillows made perfect cots for the children and Luna on the bedroom floor. As the family drifted off to sleep, lulled by the warmth and the gentle sound of the wind outside, they couldn't help but feel that this Christmas was turning into something truly special.

The first light of dawn filtered through the windows of the cabin, casting a serene glow over everything. The Johnson family stirred awake, feeling more rested than they had in a long time. Emily peeked outside and was greeted by a winter wonderland bathed in the soft light of morning. The storm had passed, leaving behind a breathtaking landscape of snow-covered trees and a clear, bright sky.

As they prepared to leave, thanking Nick for his incredible hospitality, Tom went outside to check on their car. To his amazement, he found it not only cleared of snow but also with the engine running and warm, parked right in front of the cabin. It seemed impossible given the circumstances of last night.

Nick just winked and said, "Christmas magic works in mysterious ways."

As they drove away, the family began to piece together the extraordinary events of the night. The way Nick had appeared just when they needed help, the magical aura of the cabin, and now their car, miraculously ready for their journey. It dawned on them that Nick might have been more than just a kind woodsman. The twinkle in his eye, his jovial laugh, the unexplained occurrences - could he have been Santa Claus himself?

The realization filled the car with an air of wonder and excitement. The magic of Christmas, which they had always cherished in stories, had come alive in the most unexpected way. They were leaving with more than just grateful hearts; they were carrying with them a renewed belief in the magic of the season.

Finally, the Johnson family arrived in Harmony, their hearts full of joy and eyes sparkling with the remnants of last night's magic. Grandma and Grandpa were overjoyed to see them, surprised and delighted by their unexpected arrival on Christmas morning.

As they gathered in the cozy living room, the family shared the tale of their adventurous journey and the mysterious Nick. Their grandparents listened in awe, occasionally exchanging knowing glances and smiles. The story brought everyone closer, weaving a new thread of magic into the family's Christmas traditions.

The house was filled with the aromas of delicious holiday cooking, the warmth of shared laughter, and the glow of Christmas lights. They spent the day exchanging gifts, singing carols, and reveling in the joy of being together.

As they sat down for dinner, Tom raised a toast. "To family, to the magic of Christmas, and to the mysterious ways in which life surprises us. May we always find joy in the journey, no matter where it takes us."

The toast was met with a chorus of cheers. The room brimmed with love, gratitude, and the undeniable magic of the holiday season. This Christmas, they had not only reached their destination but had also discovered the true essence of the holiday spirit.

Outside, the snow began to fall again, gently covering the world in a blanket of white. Inside, the Johnson family celebrated, their hearts warm with the magic of a Christmas they would never forget.

Chapter 32

Maggie's Delights Bakery

In the charming village of Barrington, Illinois, snowflakes gently danced in the air, dusting the streets and historic buildings with a thin layer of white. The air was brisk and sharp, hinting of the Holidays just around the corner.

Erin, a recently divorced mother, stood outside the quaint bakery she had just inherited from her beloved Aunt Maggie. Her eyes, a mirror of mixed emotions, surveyed the old-fashioned sign swinging above the door, reading "Maggie's Delights." Her heart was heavy with grief and the daunting thought of new responsibilities.

Inside, the bakery was a capsule of yesteryears. The walls, adorned with vintage baking tools and framed black-and-white photos, exuded a warmth that was both comforting and overwhelming. Erin's children, Chloe and Jayden, were exploring the nooks and crannies with wide-eyed wonder.

"Mom, look at this mixer! It's so old-timey," exclaimed Chloe, her hands gently caressing the antique appliance.

Erin smiled faintly. "Your Aunt Maggie used to bake her famous apple pies with that," she reminisced, her voice tinged with nostalgia.

Jayden, with his usual ten-year-old curiosity, was peeking into every jar and tin he could find. "Can we bake some cookies, Mom? Aunt Maggie's recipes are all here!" he said, holding up a well-worn recipe book as if it was a treasure.

Erin sighed, feeling the weight of the decision on her shoulders. "Kids, I don't know if we can keep the bakery. Running it is a huge responsibility, and I..."

"Mom, this place is special. Remember how Aunt Maggie would let us decorate our own gingerbread house every Christmas?" Chloe interjected, her eyes sparkling with memories.

"And the hot cocoa with those giant marshmallows!" added Jayden, his face lighting up.

Erin's heart swelled as she listened to her children. Their enthusiasm was infectious, but she was scared. Scared of failing, scared of letting them down.

"Kids, I'm not sure I can do this alone," Erin confessed, her voice quivering slightly.

"You're not alone, Mom. We're a team!" Chloe said, taking her mother's hand.

Jayden nodded vigorously. "Yeah, we can learn together! It'll be like our own Christmas adventure."

Their words, simple yet powerful, began to dissolve Erin's doubts. She looked around the bakery, each corner whispering stories of the past, each recipe card promising new memories. Her children's faces, filled with hope and excitement, were the nudge she needed.

"Alright, let's give it a try. For Aunt Maggie, for us," Erin declared, a newfound determination in her voice.

As the first chapter of their new journey began, the bakery, once a silent witness to many seasons, buzzed with the promise of laughter, love, and the sweet scent of fresh beginnings. Erin, Chloe, and Jayden, hand in hand, stepped into the heart of what was to become their family's legacy, kindled by the magic of Christmas and the warmth of cherished memories.

The morning sun peeked through the frosted windows of Maggie's Delights, casting a warm glow on the bustling bakery. Erin, Chloe, and Jayden had been working tirelessly since the crack of dawn, their aprons dusted with flour and faces beaming with determination.

"Mom, I think I've almost perfected Aunt Maggie's cinnamon roll recipe," Chloe announced proudly, placing a tray of golden-brown rolls onto the counter.

Erin smiled, admiring her daughter's newfound confidence in baking. "They look wonderful, Chloe! Your aunt would be so proud."

Jayden, on the other hand, was busily arranging a display of cookies by the window. "We need to catch people's attention! How about a sign that says 'World's Best Cookies Inside'?"

Erin chuckled. "That's very ambitious, Jayden. But I love your enthusiasm."

Their days were long and often challenging. Learning the ropes of running a bakery was no small feat. Erin struggled with managing finances, often staying up late poring over books and bills. But Chloe and Jayden were always there, offering help or simply a hug when needed.

Helping out at Maggie's Delights Bakery was becoming more than just a challenge for Erin's enthusiastic children, it was slowly morphing into a genuine passion. Chloe's baking skills flourished, and Jayden's quirky marketing ideas, like a "Cookie of the Day" chalkboard, drew in more customers.

One particularly busy afternoon, as the snow outside began to flurry, an elderly man entered the bakery. His eyes, wise and kind, scanned the room with a sense of familiarity.

"Good afternoon! Welcome to Maggie's Delights," Erin greeted him.

The man smiled. "Thank you, dear. I'm Mr. Nguyen. I've been coming to this bakery for more years than I can count. Maggie was a dear friend of mine."

Erin's interest was piqued. "Please, have a seat, Mr. Nguyen. Can I get you something? A coffee, perhaps?"

As Mr. Nguyen settled down with a steaming cup of coffee and a slice of apple pie, he began to share stories of the bakery's past. "Maggie had a heart of gold," he reminisced. "She would bake extra loaves of bread for those in need every Christmas. This place was more than a bakery to many."

Chloe and Jayden listened, captivated by Mr. Nguyen' tales. They looked at their mother, their eyes reflecting a shared thought.

"Mom, can we do something like that this Christmas?" Chloe asked, her voice filled with hope.

Erin nodded, touched by the idea. "Yes, we can continue Aunt Maggie's tradition. Let's bake extra pastries for those in need."

"We could even throw a party, and invite everyone over to the bakery!" Chloe brainstormed.

Jayden, ever the creative thinker, suggested, "Let's make a big banner! Something like, 'Join us for a Christmas Eve Party at Maggie's Delights!'"

Erin loved the idea. She reached out to the local food

shelf and invited them to spread the word. "Let's make this a Christmas to remember for everyone," she said with a smile.

The festive spirit in Barrington was in full swing as Christmas Eve approached. Maggie's Delights, now a beloved fixture in the community, was alive with the cheerful hustle and bustle of the holiday season.

Erin, Chloe, and Jayden worked tirelessly, their hands and hearts dedicated to baking an array of pastries for those less fortunate. The aroma of cinnamon, ginger, and fresh bread filled the air, mingling with the sound of festive music and laughter.

"Look at all these pies and cookies!" Chloe exclaimed, her eyes sparkling with pride. "Aunt Maggie would have loved this."

As the party began, the bakery was transformed. A beautifully decorated tree stood in the corner, twinkling lights strung across the windows, and the big banner Jayden had designed was proudly displayed outside.

People from all walks of life began to trickle in, greeted by the warm smiles of Erin, Chloe, and Jayden. The bakery, once a symbol of Erin's uncertainty, was now a beacon of community and joy.

Mr. Nguyen arrived, his eyes bright with delight. "Maggie would be so proud," he said, his voice filled with emotion. "You've turned this place into something truly special."

As the evening progressed, the bakery became a hub of festive cheer. Laughter and conversation filled the room, as people savored the delicious pastries. Erin and her children moved through the crowd, chatting and serving, their hearts full of happiness.

The highlight of the evening came when Erin gathered

everyone's attention. "We have a special gift for each of you," she announced. One by one, Erin, Chloe, and Jayden handed out beautifully wrapped packages containing various pastries and a small, hand-written note of hope and encouragement.

The gratitude and joy on the faces of the recipients were overwhelming. Tears, smiles, and heartfelt thanks were shared, creating an atmosphere of genuine warmth and love.

As the night came to a close, Erin stood with Chloe and Jayden, looking out at the bakery. It was more than a building full of delicious pastries; it was a place where memories were made, where love and kindness reigned.

"This was the best Christmas ever," Chloe whispered, hugging her mother.

Jayden nodded in agreement. "We did it, Mom. We really did it."

Erin looked at her children, her heart swelling with pride and love. "We did," she agreed. "Together."

The trio stood together, gazing out the window at the quaint street, reminiscent of the countless evenings Aunt Maggie must have spent doing the same. Smiles graced their faces, hearts brimming with appreciation for the gift Aunt Maggie had given.

Deep down, they were certain the legacy of Maggie's Delights would live on, not just in their family, but in the hearts of all who walked through its doors.

Just for Laughs!

from JackAndKitty.com

Why did the snowman turn yellow?
Ask the little dog over there.

Chapter 33

Snowball's Mischief

In the heart of Fargo, North Dakota, where the winter snow blankets the streets in a serene white, the Olsen family home buzzed with excitement and anticipation. Christmas was just around the corner, and this year, they had decided to welcome a new member into their family - a puppy.

"Mom, Dad, is today the day?" asked eight-year-old Ava, her eyes sparkling with excitement as she peered out the frosty window.

"Yes, sweetheart," replied her mother, Mrs. Olsen, with a warm smile. "Today, we bring our puppy home."

The family piled into their car, driving through the snowy streets to the local animal shelter. There, amidst the barks and meows, they found their new family member - a fluffy white bundle of energy with a mischievous twinkle in his eyes.

"He's perfect," whispered Ava. "Let's name him, Snowball."

The family laughed when Snowball voiced his approval.

Letting out one adorable bark, he licked Ava's face enthusiastically, his tail wagging a mile a minute.

Bringing Snowball home was like inviting a whirlwind into their lives. The puppy's antics were endless - from chewing on the tinsel-laden Christmas tree to playfully hiding socks under the couch.

"Not my socks, Snowball!" laughed Mason, Ava's older brother, as he chased the puppy around the living room.

Mrs. Olsen watched the chaos unfold with a mixture of exasperation and amusement. "He's certainly keeping us on our toes," she said to her husband, Mr. Olsen.

"Definitely," Mr. Olsen agreed, pulling a chewed-up slipper from Snowball's mouth. "But look at them. I haven't seen the kids this happy in a long time."

As Christmas approached, Snowball's antics didn't slow down. One evening, the family found their living room in disarray - pillows torn apart, and Christmas decorations strewn all over.

"Oh Snowball, what have you done?" exclaimed Mrs. Olsen, trying to sound stern but unable to hide a smile.

"Looks like he's trying to redecorate for Christmas," chuckled Mr. Olsen, as he started picking up the pieces.

Amidst the mild chaos, something special was happening. The family was spending more time together - playing with Snowball, cleaning up his messes, and laughing at his adorable mischief.

One night, as they sat together sipping hot cocoa, Ava looked up at her parents with earnest eyes. "Snowball is the best Christmas present ever. He's made everything more fun!"

Her words echoed the sentiments of the entire family. Snowball, with his boundless energy and love for life, had reminded them of the joy and spontaneity that life could offer. The Christmas spirit was truly alive in their home, not just in the decorations and the festive preparations, but in the laughter and love that filled every corner.

The soft snowfall had turned Fargo into a winter wonderland, with the Christmas spirit palpable in the air. The Olsen family, however, faced a heart-wrenching situation. A few days before Christmas, during the frenzy of holiday preparations, Snowball, their beloved puppy, had slipped out unnoticed through an open door.

"Snowball! Snowball!" Ava's voice echoed through the neighborhood as she frantically searched for her furry friend, her parents right behind her, calling out into the snowy evening.

"Don't worry, Ava. We'll find him," Mr. Olsen reassured her, though his voice betrayed his concern.

Mrs. Olsen, wrapped in her winter coat, knocked on their neighbors' doors, asking if anyone had seen a small, white puppy. The community's response was immediate and heartwarming.

"Of course, we'll keep an eye out, Mrs. Olsen," said Mr. Myers, their elderly neighbor, her own eyes brimming with worry.

As they walked through the neighborhood, the snow falling gently around them, the Olsens realized how much Snowball had already become a part of their lives. His absence left a void too big for the festive lights and decorations to fill.

"I should have been more careful with the door," Ava said, her voice small and guilt-ridden.

"Honey, it's not your fault. These things happen," Mrs. Olsen comforted her, hugging her tightly.

Their search took them to the local park, a place Snowball loved. They called out his name, hoping for a bark in response, but the park remained silent except for the soft crunch of snow under their feet.

As they searched, more community members joined in. Mrs. Sanders, the local baker, offered to put up flyers in her shop window. Teenagers from the high school volunteered to post about Snowball on social media.

"This town really comes together in times of need," Mr. Olsen observed, grateful for their neighbors' kindness.

Night fell, and with it, the temperature dropped. The family returned home, disheartened and worried. The house felt empty without Snowball's energetic presence.

Sitting by the fireplace, the family tried to maintain their Christmas spirit, but the joy of the season was overshadowed by worry for their lost puppy.

"We can't give up," said Mason, determined. "Snowball is part of our family. We'll find him, no matter what it takes."

Mrs. Olsen nodded, tears in her eyes. "He's out there somewhere, probably just as scared and cold as we are sad. We won't stop looking until we find him."

That night, as they went to bed, the Olsen family made a silent wish - for Snowball to be safe and to return home soon. The magic of Christmas, they hoped, would bring their beloved mischief maker back to them.

Christmas Eve in Fargo had a different feel this year for the Olsen family. The festive lights and decorations around the neighborhood couldn't fully lift the somber mood in their home, shadowed by the absence of their beloved puppy, Snowball.

As they sat quietly in the living room, not quite in the mood to celebrate, the phone rang, slicing through the silence with a promise of hope. Mrs. Olsen quickly answered, her voice trembling with anticipation.

"Hello, is this the Olsen family? I believe I have your puppy. Found him wandering near my backyard," a gentle voice spoke from the other end.

Tears of joy and relief filled Mrs. Olsen's eyes as she responded, "Yes, yes, that's our Snowball! We'll be right there!"

The family, filled with renewed energy, wrapped themselves in warm coats and scarves, and drove through the snow-laden streets of Fargo. Following the kind stranger's directions, they arrived at a quaint, warmly lit house on the outskirts of town.

There, in the front yard, was Snowball, his tail wagging in excitement at the sight of his family. Ava rushed out of the car and scooped him into her arms, her laughter mingling with Snowball's joyful barks.

"Thank you so much for finding him," Mr. Olsen said gratefully to the stranger, an elderly woman with a kind face.

"It's my pleasure. I'm just glad he's safe. Please, come in and warm up. I was just about to have my Christmas Eve dinner," the woman offered, her eyes twinkling with warmth.

Hesitant at first, but touched by her generosity, the family accepted her invitation. Inside the cozy home, they were greeted with the aroma of a freshly cooked meal and the sight of a beautifully decorated Christmas tree.

"I'm Doris," the woman introduced himself as they sat down at the dining table. "I live here alone, and it's a joy to have company, especially on Christmas Eve."

As they shared the meal, Doris told them stories of her own childhood in Fargo, of winters spent sledding and skating. The family, in turn, shared their own traditions and the story of how Snowball came into their lives.

"It feels like we were meant to be here tonight," Mrs. Olsen said, smiling at Doris. "This is the most unexpected Christmas Eve we've ever had."

The evening passed with laughter and heartfelt conversations. Snowball, happily curled up by the fireplace, seemed to sense that he was the reason for this special gathering.

As they prepared to leave, Doris handed them a small, wrapped gift. "A little something for Snowball," she said, winking.

Outside, the snow continued to fall gently, covering the world in a blanket of white. The Olsen family, with Snowball safely in tow, felt an overwhelming sense of gratitude for the unexpected kindness they had received.

"This is a Christmas I'll always remember," Mr. Olsen said as they drove home, the lights of Fargo twinkling around the city.

"We'll *all* remember the day you came home safely. Right, Snowball?" Ava added, hugging Snowball close.

That night, as they settled in their home, the Olsen family knew they had experienced something magical. A Christmas Eve that began with worry and sadness had transformed into an evening of warmth, kindness, and new friendships. It was a reminder that sometimes, the most precious gifts come in unexpected ways.

"Anything you can imagine you can
make real."

Jules Verne

Chapter 34

The Magic Classroom

In the heart of Sioux Falls, as winter's chill wrapped the city in a blanket of snow, Laura Perez stood by the window of her elementary school classroom, gazing out at the children playing in the yard. The laughter and shouts of joy seemed distant to her, as though they were sounds from another world. She was a dedicated teacher, known for her creativity and kindness, but lately, an overwhelming sense of exhaustion had taken hold.

The classroom was festooned with colorful Christmas decorations, paper snowflakes hanging from the ceiling, and a small artificial tree in the corner. Yet, the festive atmosphere felt forced to Laura. Her heart wasn't in it this year. The demands of teaching, the endless paperwork, and the challenge of keeping her students engaged had sapped her energy.

As the bell rang, signaling the end of recess, the children bustled back into the classroom, their cheeks rosy from the cold. They settled into their seats, chattering excitedly about the upcoming holiday break. Laura tried to muster a smile, but it didn't quite reach her eyes.

"Alright, everyone," she began, her voice lacking its usual warmth. "Let's start our Christmas craft project."

The students, sensing her lack of enthusiasm, responded half-heartedly. Laura watched them listlessly cutting out paper ornaments, and a wave of sadness washed over her. She remembered a time when teaching filled her with joy, when she felt she was making a real difference in her students' lives. But now, she questioned if that was still true.

As the day wore on, Laura felt more disconnected from her passion. The sparkle and magic of the season, which usually invigorated her teaching, now seemed like just another burden. She found herself going through the motions, her mind wandering to the days when her classroom was a place of wonder and excitement.

As the school day drew to a close, Laura sat at her desk, surrounded by half-finished Christmas crafts and ungraded papers. She looked at the smiling faces in the photos on her desk – snapshots of past classes, field trips, and happy moments. A tear slid down her cheek as she whispered to herself, "Am I really making a difference anymore?"

The room was quiet, save for the soft ticking of the clock on the wall. Laura felt a deep longing for something to reignite the passion she once had for teaching, but in that moment, it felt like an impossible wish. Little did she know, a small act of kindness was about to reawaken the joy she thought she had lost, and remind her of the true spirit of the Christmas season.

As the days edged closer to Christmas, Laura continued to feel the weight of her weariness. Each morning, she walked into her classroom with a heavy heart, trying to find the enthusiasm she once had. The festive decorations around the school seemed to mock her dwindling spirit.

However, amidst her struggles, Laura started to notice something unusual. One of her students, Liam, a quiet boy with a gentle smile, had been staying back after class every day. At first, she thought he was struggling with his work, but as she watched him, she realized he was working on something else entirely.

Curiosity piqued, Laura approached Liam one afternoon as he stayed behind again. "Liam, is everything alright? Do you need help with anything?" she asked gently.

Liam looked up, his eyes shining with a mixture of nervousness and excitement. "No, Ms. Perez, I'm fine. I'm just working on a Christmas gift," he replied.

"For your family?" Laura asked, smiling.

Liam shook his head, "No, it's for you."

Laura was taken aback. She watched as Liam carefully crafted something out of paper and glue, his small fingers working diligently. It was a handmade Christmas card, beautifully decorated with intricate designs. As he handed it to her, Laura felt a surge of emotion.

"Thank you, Liam. This means so much to me," she said, her voice cracking slightly.

Liam smiled shyly. "You're the best teacher, Ms. Perez. I wanted to make something special for you because you always help us and make learning fun."

Laura held the card close to her heart. In that moment, something shifted inside her. Liam's simple act of kindness reminded her of the reason she became a teacher. It wasn't just about lessons and grades; it was about touching lives, inspiring young minds, and nurturing hearts.

Over the next few days, Laura's perspective began to

change. She started engaging more with her students, sharing laughs, and embracing the festive spirit. The classroom once again became a place of joy and learning, filled with the excitement of the season.

The handmade card from Liam sat proudly on her desk, a constant reminder of the impact she had on her students. Laura realized that her passion for teaching wasn't lost; it had merely been overshadowed by stress and fatigue.

As Christmas drew nearer, Laura felt a renewed sense of purpose. She began to plan special activities and lessons, infusing her teaching with the passion that Liam had rekindled in her heart. The classroom buzzed with energy and happiness, a stark contrast to the gloominess of the past weeks.

Laura's heart was full as she watched her students, her love for teaching blossoming once again. Liam's unexpected gift had not only been a beautiful gesture, but it had also been the catalyst for Laura to rediscover the joy and magic of her profession.

The last day before the Christmas break arrived, a day filled with excitement and anticipation. Laura entered her classroom with a spring in her step, the memory of Liam's gift still warming her heart. The classroom was buzzing with energy, the children eagerly awaiting the start of their holiday.

As the morning progressed, Laura noticed her students whispering and giggling amongst themselves, exchanging secretive glances. Something was going on, but she couldn't quite put her finger on it. She decided to let the mystery unfold, focusing on enjoying these final moments before the break.

As the clock neared the end of the day, Liam stood up

and addressed the class. "Ms. Perez, we have a surprise for you," he announced, his voice filled with excitement.

Before Laura could respond, the children quickly rearranged the classroom, pushing desks to the sides and setting up a makeshift stage. Laura watched, her heart pounding with anticipation and confusion.

The lights dimmed, and the children began their performance. It was a Christmas play, one they had secretly been preparing for weeks. The story was simple yet touching, about a teacher who brought the magic of Christmas to her students. Laura realized, with tears in her eyes, that the play was about her.

Each scene was filled with references to their classroom experiences, the lessons Laura had taught, and the fun they had shared. The children acted with such enthusiasm and joy, their faces beaming with pride.

As the play concluded, the children gathered around Laura, singing a Christmas carol. The emotion of the moment overwhelmed her. She realized that her influence went far beyond textbooks and assignments; she was a vital part of these children's lives, a source of joy and inspiration.

Just then, as if on cue, snow began to fall outside, visible through the classroom windows. The children rushed to see, their faces pressed against the glass, marveling at the falling flakes. Laura joined them, watching the snow blanket the world in white.

This snowfall felt miraculous, like a symbol of a fresh start. As she stood there, surrounded by her students, Laura felt a profound sense of fulfillment. She understood now the true value of her work, the impact she had on these young minds and hearts.

The day ended with laughter and hugs, the magic of the

season palpable in the air. Laura waved goodbye to her students as they left for the holidays, her heart full of gratitude and love.

"The Magic Classroom" had been more than just a play; it was a reminder of the wonders of teaching, the joys of connecting with others, and the beauty of unexpected moments. Laura looked forward to the new year with renewed passion and hope, ready to continue her journey as a teacher, guided by the lessons of this magical Christmas.

"Behold, the Lamb of God, who takes
away the sin of the world!"

John 1:29

Chapter 35

A Musical Tradition That Warms the Heart

In this delightful travel essay, author Jack Norton offers a glimpse into a cherished holiday tradition he shares with his wife Kitty.

* * *

Every December, as the first snowflakes begin to blanket Minnesota's picturesque landscapes, my wife Kitty and I embark on a heartwarming tradition – attending the St. Olaf Christmas Festival. This festival, a beacon of musical excellence and holiday spirit, has become an integral part of our Christmas each year.

"Jack, do you remember our first festival?" Kitty often reminisces as we pack our winter essentials.

"Of course," I reply, smiling. "It was like stepping into a Christmas card. The whole experience was magical."

The St. Olaf Christmas Festival, a tradition dating back to 1912, began with the visionary F. Melius Christiansen. It has since grown into a global choral phenomenon. The first time we attended, we were captivated by the harmonious blend of over 500 voices, echoing through the grand hall.

"I still get goosebumps thinking about it," Kitty says, recalling the powerful, resonant sound of the choirs. "Each choir brought something unique. The St. Olaf Choir, Cantorei, Chapel Choir, Viking Chorus, Manitou Singers – each one was a thread in a beautiful tapestry of music."

As we drive to the charming town of Northfield, the scenic home of this musical jewel, we often discuss the festival's rich history. From its humble beginnings in Hoyme Memorial Chapel to the grandeur of its current setting, this festival has overcome challenges like World War II and evolved under various leaders, including Olaf Christiansen, Kenneth Jennings, and Anton Armstrong.

"Isn't it amazing how it's been televised since 1975?" I muse. "It's like sharing a piece of Minnesota with the world."

Kitty nods. "And think about its future – alternating between Orchestra Hall in Minneapolis and St. Olaf College. It's a blend of the new and the traditional."

As we stroll through Northfield, with its 150 years of history, we're always struck by the town's charm. "It's not just the festival, but this whole town that makes our tradition special," Kitty points out. "The scenic trails, the vibrant music scene, the cozy dining spots – it's all part of the experience."

Once we're settled in our seats, the lights dim, and the first notes of the choir fill the air, we're transported to a realm of peace and joy. It's a reminder of the unifying power of music, especially during the holiday season.

"This is what Christmas is all about," Kitty whispers, as the music swells.

I nod, holding her hand. "It's about tradition, community, and the joy of shared experiences."

As the final notes linger in the air, and we join the applause, our hearts are full. The St. Olaf Christmas Festival is more than just a concert; it's a journey through time, a celebration of the enduring spirit of Christmas, and a reminder of the things that truly matter – love, music, and togetherness.

This tradition is our annual pilgrimage, a cherished part of our Christmas, and a story we love to share – a reminder that in the heart of Minnesota, there's a musical wonder that brings the holiday spirit to life, year after year.

To learn more about how you can experience this incredible holiday concert, visit our travel blog: JackAndKitty.com. Can't make it to our home state of Minnesota? Don't worry! We have info on how you can watch this special event on TV or listen on the radio. In some parts of the world, it's even screened at movie theaters! Talk about a Christmas spectacle!

Chapter 36

Celebrating Loved Ones

In the quiet of Christmas, take time to slow,
Amidst the snowflakes' gentle, drifting flow.
Cherish each moment, each warm, tender embrace,
In the soft glow of lights, find love's true grace.

Gather 'round the fire, with those dear to the heart,
Share stories and laughter, let the rush depart.
In this season of giving, let love be your guide,
Celebrate loved ones, with joy amplified.

Chapter 37

Once Upon a Snowy Encounter

The first snowfall of the season had blanketed Minneapolis in a pristine layer of white, transforming the city into a winter wonderland. But for Michelle, a young marketing executive at a bustling downtown firm, the picturesque scenery was just a fleeting backdrop to her hectic life.

It was the week before Christmas, and the city was alive with holiday cheer. Twinkling lights adorned the streets, and the air was filled with the sound of carolers and the scent of freshly baked gingerbread. Yet, amidst this festive atmosphere, Michelle felt a sense of overwhelm.

Her days were a whirlwind of meetings, deadlines, and endless emails. She often worked late, her office overlooking the glittering cityscape, a silent witness to her dedication. Michelle had always been ambitious, climbing the corporate ladder with a tenacity that left little room for anything else, especially not dating.

Her friends often joked that her laptop was her significant other, and she laughed it off, but deep down, she felt a pang of loneliness. She missed the simpler times, the days when Christmas meant family gatherings, homemade cookies, and watching classic holiday movies.

As she walked briskly through the snowy streets of Minneapolis, her mind was preoccupied with the upcoming office holiday party. She had volunteered to pick up the catered meal, a task she now regretted, given her already packed schedule.

As she neared the local deli, known for its delicious holiday spreads, her phone buzzed relentlessly with work notifications. Michelle sighed, longing for a moment of peace amid the chaos.

Entering the deli, she was greeted by the warm aroma of roasted turkey and cinnamon. The place was bustling with people, all in a rush to prepare for their own holiday celebrations. Michelle joined the line, her thoughts drifting to the Christmases of her past, a nostalgic smile touching her lips.

Little did she know, a chance encounter was about to unfold, one that would remind her of the joys she had been missing in her relentless pursuit of career success. This encounter would be the beginning of a heartwarming journey, one that would rekindle the magic of the season in her heart.

Michelle was meticulously checking her order at the deli counter when a familiar voice startled her. "Michelle? Michelle Thompson, is that you?" She turned around to see a face from her past, one she hadn't seen in well over a decade.

Standing there, with a warm smile and a slightly graying hairline, was Alex Hughes, her old high school classmate. He looked different, yet his eyes still held the same playful sparkle she remembered.

"Alex! Wow, I can't believe it's you!" Michelle exclaimed,

her surprise evident. The hustle of the deli faded into the background as they shared a moment of disbelief at their unexpected reunion.

They stepped aside, allowing others to pass, and started catching up. Alex shared that he had become a high school teacher, teaching history, his favorite subject back in the day. He spoke with a passion that was infectious, his eyes lighting up as he described his work with the students.

Michelle listened, feeling a mix of admiration and a pang of envy for his apparent contentment in life. She shared her own journey, painting a picture of her corporate life, the successes, and the stresses. As she spoke, she realized how much she missed having conversations that weren't about work or business.

Their conversation flowed effortlessly, the years melting away as they reminisced about their high school days. They laughed over fond memories of school events, mutual friends, and shared classes.

Time seemed to stand still, and before they knew it, an hour had passed. Michelle glanced at her watch in panic, realizing she was running late. Alex, noticing her sudden anxiety, offered to help her carry the food back to her office.

As they walked through the snowy streets of Minneapolis, carrying the trays of holiday fare between them, Michelle felt a lightness she hadn't experienced in a long time. The burden of her responsibilities seemed to lift slightly, replaced by a sense of connection and joy.

Their conversation continued, filled with laughter and ease. Alex's easygoing nature was a soothing balm to Michelle's frazzled state. It was refreshing to be around someone who wasn't absorbed in the fast-paced corporate world, someone who appreciated the simpler things in life.

As they reached her office building, Michelle thanked Alex for his help and company. There was a moment of hesitation, a lingering look, and then Alex suggested, "Maybe we could catch up over coffee sometime?"

Michelle smiled, feeling a flicker of excitement at the prospect. "I'd like that," she replied.

They exchanged numbers, and as Alex walked away, Michelle watched him go, feeling a warmth in her heart that had been absent for too long. This chance encounter, she thought, might just be the beginning of something new and unexpected.

The coffee date between Michelle and Alex took place on a chilly December evening. The city of Minneapolis was aglow with holiday lights, casting a festive shimmer over the snow-covered streets. As they sat in the quaint coffee shop, sipping on warm drinks, the conversation flowed as smoothly as it had at the deli.

Feeling adventurous, they decided to take a stroll through the city to enjoy the holiday decorations. The streets were bustling with people, families enjoying the season, couples walking hand in hand, and the sound of laughter filled the air. Michelle felt a sense of wonder she hadn't experienced in years.

As they walked, they stumbled upon a charity event in a local park. Volunteers were gathered around a large Christmas tree, handing out gifts to underprivileged children. The sight was touching, and the joy on the children's faces was palpable. Moved by the scene, Michelle and Alex decided to lend a hand.

They approached the organizers and were soon helping distribute gifts. Michelle found herself deeply affected by the experience, her heart swelling with every child's smile and laugh. It was a stark contrast to her usual world of deadlines and meetings.

Then, something extraordinary happened. As Michelle handed a wrapped gift to a little girl, she noticed the wrapping paper – it was the same unique pattern she had chosen for a gift donation years ago when she was a child. She remembered the wrapping paper vividly, it was a print of a dog and snowflakes, with a dog that looked remarkably similar to her beloved childhood pet, Bunson.

The dog pictured on the wrapping paper brought back memories of Bunson and her special love for the Christmas season as a child. A time when she didn't have any To-Dos or a hectic work schedule. A time in her life when she looked at the world with childlike wonder, and spent quality time with loved ones.

The realization hit her like a wave – the wrapping paper that reminded her of childhood, and her cherished memories of Bunson all those years ago, had somehow made its way back to her hands. It felt like a small miracle, a sign from the universe. She shared this remarkable coincidence with Alex, her voice filled with wonder.

Alex looked at her, his eyes reflecting the twinkling lights of the Christmas tree. "Maybe it's a reminder," he said gently, "a reminder of the simple joys, of being part of something bigger than ourselves."

That moment, under the glow of the holiday lights, amidst the laughter and cheer, Michelle felt a shift within her. She realized how caught up she had been in the fast pace of her life, forgetting to appreciate the small moments, the connections that truly mattered.

Alex and Michelle spent the rest of the evening walking through the festive streets, talking about everything and nothing. They shared stories, hopes, and laughter, the city's holiday spirit enveloping them.

As the night drew to a close, they found themselves back at the park, standing near the now quiet Christmas tree. The magic of the season, the joy of the day's events, and the rediscovery of simple pleasures had brought them closer.

Michelle looked up at Alex, her heart full of gratitude. "Thank you," she said, "for reminding me what the holidays are really about."

Alex smiled, his eyes warm. "Thank you for sharing this magical night with me," he replied.

As they parted ways, with promises to see each other soon, Michelle felt a renewed sense of joy and wonder. This unexpected reconnection with Alex had not only brought back memories of her past but had also opened her heart to the possibilities of the future.

The magic of the Christmas season had worked its charm, reminding her of the importance of slowing down, cherishing connections, and finding joy in the simplest of things. This, she realized, was the true spirit of the holidays.

As the story of Michelle and Alex's enchanting Christmas comes to a close, there's a heartwarming twist to their tale. This magical series of events, starting from a chance encounter in a deli to a night filled with joy and rediscovery, didn't happen just recently. In fact, it unfolded nearly 30 years ago.

Today, Michelle and Alex are celebrating their 27th wedding anniversary. Their life together has been a journey filled with love, laughter, and countless shared adventures. They have built a family, watched their children grow, and now delight in the laughter of their grandchildren.

Every Christmas, they reminisce about that fateful

holiday season when a simple coffee date blossomed into a lifetime of companionship. Their story has become a cherished family legend, living proof of the magic of the season and the serendipity of life.

Their grandchildren's eyes always light up when they hear about the Christmas tree charity event and the miraculous wrapping paper of her dog, Bunson, that found its way back to Grandma Michelle. It's a tale that reminds them all to cherish every moment and to believe in the magic that life holds, especially during the holiday season.

Michelle and Alex's story, born from a chance encounter one snowy December in Minneapolis, continues to inspire and warm the hearts of their family, proving that sometimes, the most unexpected moments can lead to the most beautiful destinations.

What did Adam say the day before Christmas? "It's Christmas, Eve!"

Chapter 38

The Light of Decorah

In the small, picturesque town of Decorah, Iowa, nestled amongst rolling hills and snowy landscapes, there was a house that once glowed brighter than any other during the Christmas season. This was the home of Mrs. Evelyn Hanson, a kind-hearted elderly woman known for her love of Christmas. Each year, Evelyn and her late husband, John, would transform their humble abode into a winter wonderland, complete with twinkling lights, vibrant wreaths, and an array of festive ornaments that captured the joy of the season.

Evelyn and John were more than just life partners; they were Christmas enthusiasts who shared a deep passion for the holiday's magic. Together, they would meticulously plan their decorations, adding new pieces each year, and their house became a beloved holiday landmark in Decorah. Neighbors and passersby would stop to admire the spectacle, often leaving with brighter spirits and warmer hearts.

But since John's passing, the lights had dimmed on the Hanson household. The boxes of decorations, once eagerly unpacked each year, now lay forgotten in the attic, gathering dust and memories. Without her beloved John, Evelyn couldn't find the strength to celebrate. The joy they shared seemed to have faded away with him, leaving her in a world that felt colder and less colorful.

As the years went by, Evelyn's once vibrant spirit seemed to wane with the absence of the festive cheer. The Christmas season, which had been a time of warmth and togetherness, now served as a reminder of her profound loss. The laughter and music that once filled her home were replaced by silence, and the twinkling lights gave way to the somber shadows of winter.

Yet, despite her solitude, Evelyn held onto the memories of those joyous Christmases spent with John. She would often sit by the window, sipping her tea, gazing out at the snow-covered streets of Decorah, reminiscing about the times when her home was the heart of Christmas in their little town. Those memories, both sweet and poignant, were now the only connection she had to the Christmases of the past.

As another Christmas season approached, the town of Decorah buzzed with excitement. Streets were lined with festive lights, shop windows displayed holiday scenes, and the sound of carols filled the air. The entire town seemed to be wrapped in a blanket of joy and anticipation, all except for one house — the Hanson residence.

Evelyn watched from her window as her neighbors adorned their homes with decorations, children played in the snow, and families prepared for the upcoming holiday festivities. But inside her house, time seemed to stand still. The walls echoed with the silence of solitude, and the lack of festive decor made it feel even more empty.

Her friends and neighbors often expressed their concerns for her. They missed the bright lights and the festive spirit that once emanated from her home. They tried to encourage her to join the holiday celebrations, to rekindle the joy she once felt, but Evelyn politely declined. They understood her grief and respected her need for solitude, though it pained them to see her so withdrawn.

As the days grew shorter and the nights colder, Evelyn's sense of loneliness deepened. The cheerful holiday music that filtered through her walls from the outside world only served as a stark reminder of her isolation. The Christmas spirit, which once filled her heart and home, now seemed like a distant dream, out of reach and lost in the past.

Inside her quiet home, amidst the shadows of fading memories, Evelyn longed for the warmth and love that Christmas once brought her. But without John, the holiday season felt empty and devoid of meaning. The joy and excitement that once surrounded her seemed to have vanished, leaving her in a world that was a little less bright and a little less hopeful.

As Christmas break approached, the town of Decorah prepared to celebrate with more fervor than ever. Little did Evelyn know, this Christmas would be different. A group of kind-hearted teenagers, led by a compassionate soul named Lacey, had a special plan in mind, a plan that would bring light back to the Hanson household and reawaken the spirit of Christmas in Evelyn's heart.

In the heart of Decorah, at the local high school, a group of friends gathered in the bustling cafeteria before the holiday break, the air thick with the chatter and laughter typical of the festive season. Among them was Lacey, a kind-hearted and spirited teenager known for her infectious enthusiasm and compassion.

As they exchanged stories about their holiday plans, Lacey's gaze drifted out the window. She thought about her daily drive to school, and how much she missed seeing the Hanson's house so festively decorated. It was something she had come to look forward to every year for as long as she could remember.

Now, it just made her sad. The quiet, undecorated house of Mrs. Hanson made life seem unfair. Especially for someone who'd always gone out of her way to make the whole town excited for the Christmas.

A sense of concern washed over Lacey as she thought about the lonely widow. She remembered the magnificent Christmas displays that once graced Mrs. Hanson's home. It saddened her to see such a stark contrast now — a home once filled with light and joy, now shadowed and silent.

With a determined look, Lacey turned to her friends. "Guys, I have an idea," she said, her eyes sparkling with a mixture of excitement and empathy. "What if we help Mrs. Hanson decorate her house this Christmas? Maybe we can bring some holiday cheer back into her life."

Her friends, initially surprised by the suggestion, quickly warmed up to the idea. They all knew of Mrs. Hanson and her legendary Christmas displays. The thought of helping her, of bringing a bit of joy to someone who had lost so much, ignited a sense of purpose in them.

Over the next few days, Lacey and her friends put their plan into action. They gathered decorations from their homes, pooling together strings of lights, garlands, and even a miniature but beautiful artificial Christmas tree. They planned every detail with care and excitement, determined to make this a Christmas Eve that Mrs. Hanson would never forget.

As Christmas Eve approached, the group's excitement grew. They wrapped up their final preparations, each of them feeling a profound sense of anticipation and joy at the thought of bringing some light to Mrs. Hanson's holiday.

The evening of Christmas Eve arrived, a blanket of fresh snow covering the streets of Decorah, reflecting the twinkling lights from the decorated houses. Inside her home, Evelyn sat quietly, a cup of tea in her hands, lost in memories of Christmases past.

Then, there was a knock at the door. Startled, Evelyn hesitated. It was unusual for her to have visitors, especially on Christmas Eve. Curiosity mingled with trepidation as she made her way to the door, her heart beating a little faster.

When she opened the door, she was met with the sight of Lacey and her friends, their faces beaming with excitement and kindness. In their hands, they held boxes of decorations and the miniature artificial Christmas tree.

"Mrs. Hanson," Lacey began, her voice filled with warmth, "we thought you might like some company and a bit of holiday cheer this Christmas Eve. We've brought decorations and... well, we'd love to help you decorate your house, if that's okay with you."

Evelyn was taken aback, her heart touched by the gesture but her mind clouded with hesitation. She hadn't celebrated Christmas since John's passing, and the idea of decorating her home now felt almost overwhelming.

Yet, as she looked into the eager, hopeful faces of Lacey and her friends, something within her stirred. It was a flicker of warmth, a hint of the Christmas spirit that she thought she had lost forever.

With a gentle smile, Evelyn stepped aside, opening her door to the group. "Well, I suppose it wouldn't hurt to have a little bit of Christmas spirit around here," she said, her voice quivering with emotion.

As the teens stepped inside, bringing with them the decorations and a burst of youthful energy, Evelyn felt a warmth she hadn't experienced in years.

After a quick survey of the decorations, Lacey asked if she and her friends could grab the boxes and Christmas tree up in the attic.

After a few moments of indecision, Evelyn agreed. Seeing the affection in Lacey's eyes, and the genuine concern of the teens for her wellbeing, Evelyn couldn't resist. Their kindness towards her made the older woman realize this was a blessing in disguise.

The group got to work, humming tunes as they worked as a team to make the house burst with color. Evelyn joined in, unpacking the boxes with a heart full of emotion. She began to share stories of past Christmases with her husband, each ornament and decoration evoking a cherished memory.

The house slowly came to life, as strings of lights lit up the windows, the garlands adorned the walls, and the Christmas tree stood tall and proud in the living room. With each decoration, Evelyn's home felt a little less empty, and her heart a little more full.

This unexpected Christmas Eve gathering, a blend of past memories and present joy, marked the beginning of a night that would rekindle Evelyn's love for the holiday season and show her the enduring power of kindness and community.

As the evening unfolded, Evelyn's living room buzzed with activity and laughter. The group of teenagers, led by

Lacey, worked alongside Evelyn, each taking a part in bringing the festive spirit back into the house. The boxes of decorations, long untouched, were fully reorganized and unpacked, revealing treasures of Christmases past.

Evelyn, with a gentle hand, lifted each ornament, continuing to share stories with the teens. She spoke of the little glass angel she and John had found at a Christmas market on their honeymoon, the handmade decorations they had crafted during their first Christmas together, and the various trinkets they had collected over the years. Each story was a thread in the rich tapestry of her life with John, woven with love and cherished memories.

The teenagers listened intently, hanging on every word. They were captivated by Evelyn's stories, feeling as though they were glimpsing into a beautiful, bygone world. As they decorated, they began to understand the depth of Evelyn's love for John and her passion for Christmas.

Gradually, the house began to transform into a holiday wonderland. Strings of lights twinkled in the windows, casting a warm glow into the snowy night. Garlands and wreaths adorned the walls and doors, bringing life and color back into the home. The Christmas tree, once a symbol of Evelyn's lost joy, now stood tall and proud, adorned with ornaments rich in history and love.

As they decorated, something magical happened. The act of adorning her home with festive cheer, once a painful reminder of her loss, became a healing experience for Evelyn. With each ornament placed, with each story shared, her spirit seemed to grow brighter. The laughter and energy of the teens breathed new life into her and into the home that had been shrouded in silence for too long.

With the house now brimming with Christmas spirit, the

group gathered around the newly decorated tree. Its lights cast a soft, warm glow, illuminating the faces of the teens and Evelyn, who sat among them, a smile touching her lips.

Lacey, feeling a surge of joy, started humming a familiar Christmas carol. Soon, the others joined in, their voices blending in harmony. The melody filled the room, and a gentle peace settled over the group. The carols they sang were old and familiar, songs that Evelyn and John had once sung together.

Evelyn, her heart swelling with emotion, found her voice joining in. It was rusty from years of silence, but rich with emotion. The songs brought back memories, a mixture of happiness and nostalgia, and for a moment, it felt like John was right there with them, his presence felt in every note.

As the last notes of the carol faded, Lacey noticed the star, the one that Evelyn had said hadn't worked since John's passing. It lay in a box, still beautiful despite its years. With a hopeful glance at Evelyn, Lacey suggested they try placing it atop the tree.

With a tender smile, Evelyn agreed. The group watched in anticipation as Lacey carefully climbed the ladder and placed the star at the very top of the tree. For a moment, nothing happened. Then, as if by some Christmas miracle, the star flickered to life, shining brightly, casting a gentle, golden light over the room.

Gasps and smiles erupted around the room. Evelyn's eyes filled with tears of joy. In that moment, it felt as if John was sending a message, a reminder that the love they shared and the joy of Christmas were still alive, still shining brightly. It was a moment of pure magic, a testament to the enduring power of love and the miracles that the Christmas season can bring.

The lighting of the star became the crowning moment of the evening, symbolizing hope, renewal, and the endless capacity of the human heart to find joy even in the midst of sorrow. It was a moment that would stay with Evelyn and the teens for the rest of their lives, a reminder of the night when they shared not just in decorating a house, but in healing a heart.

As the star atop the tree glowed, the room fell into a hushed silence. The soft, golden light seemed to cast a spell over everyone present. For Evelyn, the illumination of the star was more than just a physical light; it was a beacon of hope, a tangible connection to her beloved John. The star's light seemed to fill the room with warmth, wrapping around her like a comforting embrace.

Evelyn's heart swelled with emotion as she gazed at the shining star. It felt as if John's spirit was there with them, smiling down upon the scene of joy and togetherness. The tears that streamed down her cheeks were no longer just of sorrow but also of joy and gratitude. In this miraculous moment, Evelyn realized that the essence of Christmas had never truly left her. The love, the joy, the warmth — it had been there all along, nestled deep within her heart, waiting for the right moment to reemerge.

The teenagers watched in awe, deeply moved by the significance of the moment. They could feel the magic in the air, a magic that went beyond the boundaries of the physical world. In this one miraculous instance, they understood the true meaning of Christmas — it was more than just lights and gifts; it was about love, memory, and the connections that bind us together across time and space.

The room was filled with a profound sense of peace and wonder. The group, once strangers, now connected by an incredible shared experience, basked in the glow of the tree and the star, feeling a sense of unity and joy that only the magic of Christmas can bring.

As the evening progressed, the miraculous lighting of the star seemed to radiate beyond the walls of Evelyn's home. Word quickly spread through the neighborhood, and soon, a small crowd of neighbors and friends gathered outside, drawn by the sight of the beautifully decorated house that once again shone brightly in the heart of Decorah.

Evelyn, stepping out onto her porch, was greeted by the smiling faces of her community. The sight of her home, alight with Christmas cheer, had touched something in everyone who came to see it. People who had not spoken in years were chatting amiably, children laughed and played in the snow, and the air was filled with the sweet sound of carols.

As she looked around at the gathering, Evelyn felt a profound sense of belonging and love. She realized that the true spirit of Christmas was not just in the decorations or the gifts; it was in the coming together of community, the sharing of joy, and the miracles, both big and small, that the season brought.

The teenagers, standing beside Evelyn, looked on with pride and happiness. They had set out to bring some holiday cheer to one person, but in doing so, they had ignited a spark of joy and unity that spread throughout the entire neighborhood. They learned firsthand the impact of kindness and the power of community, lessons they would carry with them for the rest of their lives.

As the night drew to a close, the town of Decorah was left with a heartwarming story that would be told for years to come. A story of a Christmas miracle, a reminder of the magic that the season holds, and the enduring power of love and community. In that magical Christmas season, Evelyn and the people of Decorah rediscovered the true essence of the holiday — a time of togetherness, joy, and the enduring wonder of life's unexpected miracles.

Chapter 39

Christmas Cookie Mix-Up

Once upon a time in Akron, Ohio, there was a young boy named Grayson, who was brimming with holiday excitement. Grayson had a plan: to bake the sweetest sugar cookies for Santa Claus. He had been practicing all year, and now, Christmas Eve had arrived.

"Mom, today's the big day! Santa's going to love these!" Grayson exclaimed, his eyes sparkling with excitement.

His mother smiled warmly. "I'm sure he will, honey. Let's get started!"

In the cozy kitchen, Grayson and his mom began mixing ingredients. Flour, eggs, butter – everything was going perfectly until Grayson reached for the sugar jar. Distracted by his excitement, he accidentally grabbed the salt container instead.

"Mom, do we just dump all the sugar in?" Grayson asked innocently.

"Yes, but be careful. We want them just right for Santa," she replied, attending to the oven.

Grayson poured the 'sugar' into the bowl, and they mixed and shaped the cookies together, placing them in the oven with care.

As the cookies baked, Grayson's father came in, whistling Christmas tunes. "Something smells good! Grayson's famous cookies, I presume?"

Grayson beamed. "The best batch ever!"

Soon, the timer dinged, and they all gathered around to see the results. The cookies were golden and perfectly shaped. Grayson, bursting with pride, offered the first cookie to his parents.

His mom's smile faltered at the first bite, and his dad tried to hide his surprise. The cookies were salty, not sweet!

Grayson's face fell. "Aren't they good?" he asked, his voice quivering.

His parents exchanged a glance, then his father chuckled softly. "You know, I think Santa might enjoy something a bit different this year."

His mother nodded. "Absolutely! Santa has so many sweet cookies. Yours will stand out, Grayson!"

Grayson's spirits lifted. "You really think so?"

"Yes!" his father said, giving him a reassuring hug. "And it's the thought that counts most."

That night, as they set the salty cookies out for Santa, Grayson felt a warm glow in his heart. Maybe the cookies weren't perfect, but he knew his effort was what truly mattered.

In the morning, Grayson rushed to the living room, finding a thank you note from Santa. "Dear Grayson, thank you for the unique cookies! They were a delightful surprise. Keep baking and spreading joy. Merry Christmas!"

Grayson's eyes shone with happiness. He had given

Santa a Christmas surprise, and in return, Santa had given him the gift of confidence and the joy of giving.

And so, in a small kitchen in Akron, Ohio, a batch of salty cookies brought a family closer, teaching them that it's not just the ingredients that make the holidays special, but the love and laughter shared in every moment.

What do you call chess players bragging about their games in a hotel lobby? Chess nuts boasting in an open foyer.

Chapter 40

The Magical Wooden Horse

The winter of 1933 in Pella, Iowa, was harsh, especially for the Beyer family, living in a modest farmhouse on the outskirts of town. Once prosperous farmers, the Great Depression had taken its toll on them. The barn stood half-empty, and the fields lay fallow, a stark contrast to the bountiful years gone by.

Inside, the house was modest but filled with love. 10-year-old Charlie, with his mop of curly hair and wide, curious eyes, was the youngest of three. He spent his days exploring every nook and cranny of the old farmhouse, looking for hidden treasures or secret passageways.

One cold December day, as a gentle snow began to fall, Charlie ventured into the attic. It was a place he rarely went, filled with relics of better times. Amidst the dust-covered furniture and boxes of forgotten memories, Charlie's eyes landed on something extraordinary: a beautifully crafted, antique wooden horse. It had intricately carved details and a mane that seemed to flow like real hair.

"Wow," Charlie whispered, running his fingers over the smooth wood. "You're beautiful."

He rushed downstairs, the toy horse cradled in his arms, to show his family. His mother, Mildred, was in the kitchen, trying to make the most out of their meager rations, while his father, George, sat by the fireplace, his face etched with the worries of the world.

"Look what I found!" Charlie exclaimed, bursting into the room.

Mildred turned, her weary face lighting up with a smile. "Oh, Charlie, that's wonderful! Where did you find it?"

"In the attic!" he said, his eyes shining with excitement.

George looked up, his interest piqued. "That's a fine toy, son. I haven't seen that in years. It belonged to your grandfather."

Charlie sat down next to his father, the horse between them. "Tell me about Grandpa," he urged, eager to hear stories of happier times.

As George began to recount tales of his father, a sense of warmth filled the room. Mildred joined them, bringing warm milk, and soon they were all laughing and sharing stories. The wooden horse, now placed at the center of the hearth, seemed to glow in the firelight.

"This was your grandpa's favorite toy," George said, his voice softening. "He believed it brought good luck."

"Maybe it can bring us luck too," Charlie said, more to the horse than to anyone else.

That Christmas Eve, despite the hardship and the cold, the Beyer family knew that somehow they would be okay. They always had each other.

The night grew late, and as Charlie drifted to sleep on

the floor by the fire, he hugged the wooden horse tight. Thinking about his grandpa hugging this very same lucky toy, he felt an inexplicable sense of comfort and peace. Outside, the snow continued to fall softly, blanketing Pella in a serene white, as if the world itself was hushing to listen to the heartbeat of a family rediscovering joy in the simplest of things.

In the bustling town of Pella, Iowa, the 1980s had brought change, but not all of it was good. The economic recession had left its mark, and many families found themselves struggling to make ends meet.

Nancy, a single mother working two jobs, tried her best to provide for her children, Lisa and Tony. They lived in a small apartment on the edge of town, filled with love, but sparse in luxuries.

One chilly December afternoon, Nancy took Lisa and Tony to a local thrift store, hoping to find some affordable winter clothes. Lisa, a bright-eyed girl of eight, wandered through the aisles, her younger brother Tony in tow.

"Mom, look!" Lisa called out, her voice echoing slightly in the quiet store.

Nancy, browsing through a rack of coats, turned to see what had caught her daughter's attention. There, on a dusty shelf, lay an antique wooden horse, its paint faded but its craftsmanship unmistakable.

"It's beautiful," Lisa breathed, gently lifting the toy. She stroked its golden mane, stiffened by time.

Nancy came over, a smile tugging at her lips. "It's very old, honey. Someone must have cherished it once."

"Can we get it, Mom? Please?" Lisa's eyes were wide with hope.

Looking at the price tag, Nancy hesitated. It was affordable, but every dollar counted. She saw the longing in her children's eyes and nodded. "Alright, but it's an early Christmas gift."

At home, the toy horse took a place of honor on the mantle. Lisa and Tony would often play with it, creating fantastical stories of knights and adventures. Nancy noticed a change in the atmosphere of their home; it felt warmer, more cheerful.

A week before Christmas, Nancy received a call. It was from a company she had applied to months ago. They offered her a job, one with better pay and hours.

"I got the job!" she exclaimed, hugging her children. "It's our little Christmas miracle."

As they celebrated, Lisa looked at the wooden horse, whispering, "Thank you."

Christmas Eve arrived, and they were invited to a neighborhood gathering. It was there that Lisa and Tony made new friends, other kids from the area who welcomed them with open arms.

Sitting around the fire that night, Nancy shared the story of the toy horse with her new friends, her children nestled close to her. The room was filled with laughter and the warmth of community.

"It's more than just a toy," Nancy thought, looking at the horse. "It's like it's brought us luck, happiness."

Lisa, snuggled against her, smiled and said, "It's magical, Mom. It's our magic horse."

As they left the gathering, their hearts full of joy and the promise of better days, the snow began to fall gently. Pella, with its twinkling lights and the soft white blanket of snow, seemed to be celebrating with them.

The antique wooden horse, now a beloved part of their family, stood silently, a gentle smile carved on its face.

In present-day Pella, life had evolved but the small-town charm remained intact. Don and Ginny, an elderly couple, had recently settled into a cozy retirement home, their lives quieter now, yet filled with rich memories of days gone by.

Their grandson, Ian, a college student with a heart full of curiosity, visited them one chilly December day. He brought with him a peculiar gift he had stumbled upon at a local flea market – an antique wooden horse, beautifully crafted and seemingly from another era.

"Grandma, Grandpa, look what I found," Ian said, presenting the toy with a sense of wonder.

Ginny's eyes sparkled with a sense of recognition. "Oh, Ian, it's lovely. It reminds me of a toy horse my father used to talk about from his childhood."

Don, looking over his glasses, added, "Yes, I remember hearing something about a wacky toy horse, years ago. Said to be a good-luck charm? I never believed in any of that nonsense, but that carving on that toy does look fancy. It guess it was pretty important to someone."

Their conversation sparked an idea in Ian. Why not use this toy horse as a catalyst to bring some holiday cheer to the retirement home, perhaps even reconnecting residents with cherished memories of their own?

With the help of the staff, Ian organized a Christmas party at the home. The antique toy horse was placed at the center of the festivities, its presence a silent yet powerful reminder of childhood wonder.

As the residents gathered, the horse seemed to act as a bridge, connecting them to their past. They shared stories of Christmases long ago, of toys and joys, of hardship and hope. The room buzzed with laughter and the warmth of shared memories.

Don and Ginny, watching the scene unfold, felt a renewed sense of connection to their community. They too shared their stories, their voices blending into the shared history.

"Who would have thought," Ginny mused, "that an old toy could bring us all together like this?"

Don, holding her hand, smiled. "It's the magic of memories, dear. They live on in the simplest of things. Even an old piece of carved wood."

The Christmas party became a night to remember, not just for Don and Ginny, but for all the residents of the home. The toy horse, a silent witness to the festivities, seemed to glow under the twinkling Christmas lights.

As the evening drew to a close, Ian looked at his grandparents and their friends, their faces alight with joy. He realized that the true value of the toy wasn't in its history or its magic, but in its ability to bring people together, to spark conversation and connection.

The toy horse remained in the retirement home, standing proudly on the mantle, a symbol of the timeless joy and unity that it had brought to everyone there. And as Pella continued to grow and change, the simple, beautiful toy horse remained a cherished reminder of the enduring power of community and shared memories.

Chapter 41

The Lopsided Snowman

Once upon a snowy December in La Crosse, Wisconsin, 8-year-old Connor decided to build a snowman for his parents. Bundled up in his blue jacket and white mittens, he stepped into the fresh snow, his heart filled with a mission to make the perfect snowman.

As he rolled the snow into big balls, he realized building a snowman was harder than he thought. His first attempt leaned too much to the side, and the second one fell apart. Feeling a bit discouraged, he heard his neighbor, Mrs. Duncan, call out from her porch, "Keep trying, Connor! Every snowman is special, no matter how it looks."

Renewed with determination, Connor tried again. This time, the snowman stood, albeit a little lopsided. He found sticks for arms, stones for eyes, and a carrot for the nose. But when he stepped back, Connor felt it still wasn't right.

As he pondered, his parents came outside. "What's this, Connor?" his dad asked with a smile.

"I wanted to make you the best snowman ever, but I just couldn't get it right," Connor said, his voice wavering.

His mom knelt beside him, "Oh, Connor, it's wonderful because you made it. It's the love you put into it that makes it special."

Just then, a cloud shifted, allowing sunlight to shine through, onto the snowman. Under its spotlight from the heavens, it appeared as if it were glowing softly, surprising everyone. The stones, sticks, and carrot seemed to shimmer with a magical light.

"Look, Mom, Dad! The snowman!" Connor exclaimed in awe.

His dad wrapped an arm around him. "This is the wonderful thing about Christmas, Connor. It's not about getting things perfect. It's about the love and effort you put in."

Together, they admired the glowing snowman under the bright sky. It was a simple snowman, but to Connor and his parents, it was a perfect symbol of love, effort, and the magic of Christmas.

And from that Christmas on, every snowman Connor built had a special place in their hearts, a reminder of the magic that happens when you put your heart into everything you do.

Just for Laughs!

from JackAndKitty.com

Art by Jack and Kitty Norton. Copyright 2023.

What happened when the snowgirl broke up with the snowboy? She gave him the cold shoulder.

Chapter 42

'Twas the Night Before Christmas...in Wisconsin

Grab your beer and cheese curds, because we have a poem for our cheesehead pals from Wisconsin! We hope you get a giggle from our "Badger State Version" of this classic Christmas poem.

* * *

'Twas the night before Christmas, in the Wisconsin home,
Where not even a badger was stirring, nor a gnome;
The stockings were hung by the log fire with zest,
In hopes that St. Nick would bring cheese curds, they're the best.

The children were tucked in their Green Bay Packer gear,
Dreams of snowmobiles racing brought smiles ear to ear;
And mamma in her Brewers cap, and I in my Bucks,
Had just settled down after watching some ducks.

When out on the lawn there arose such a clatter,

I sprang from the recliner to see what was the matter.
Away to the window I flew like a flash,
Spilled my Old Fashioned and made quite the splash.

The moon on the stretch of the new-fallen snow,
Lit up the yard like Lambeau's own glow,
When what to my cheese-curd-lovin' eyes did show,
But a miniature sleigh, no Packers, just snow.

With a little old driver so lively and slick,
I knew in a heartbeat it must be St. Nick.
Quicker than muskies his reindeer they came,
And he whistled, and shouted, and called them by name:

"Now, Bratwurst! now, Kringle! now, Polka and Blitzen!
On, Cheddar! on, Stout! on, Lager and Mitten!
To the top of the porch! to the top of the wall!
Now dash away! dash away! dash away all!"

As dry leaves before the wild Badger game fly,
When they meet with an obstacle, mount to the sky;
Up to the rooftop the coursers they flew,
With the sleigh full of beer, and St. Nicholas too.

And then, in a twinkling, I heard on the shingles,
The prancing and pawing of each little Kris Kringle.
As I pulled in my head, and was turning around,
Down the chimney St. Nicholas came with a bound.

He was dressed all in mink, from his head to his foot,
And his clothes were all tarnished with ashes and soot;
A bundle of toys he had flung on his back,

And he looked like a peddler just opening his pack.

His eyes—how they twinkled with mischievous cheer!
His dimples, how merry, his laugh I could hear!
His droll little mouth was drawn up in delight,
And the beard on his chin was as snowy as the night;

The stump of a cheese stick he held tight in his grin,
And the aroma of beer, it circled his chin.
He had a broad face and a round little beer belly
That shook when he chuckled, like a jar full of jelly.

He was chubby and plump, a right jolly cheesehead,
And I laughed when I saw him; I felt no dread.
A wink of his eye and a twist of his head,
Soon let me know I had nothing to dread;

He spoke not a word, but went straight to his task,
Filled all the stockings with goodies; just ask!
And laying his finger aside of his nose,
Giving a nod, up the chimney he rose.

He sprang to his sleigh, to his team gave a call,
And away they all flew, like a snowball.
But I heard him exclaim, as he drove out of sight,
"Happy Christmas to all, and to all a Wisconsin-good-night!"

Just for Laughs!

from JackAndKitty.com

If Santa and Mrs. Claus had a baby, what would he be? A subordinate Claus.

Chapter 43

The Great Snowball Fight of Hayward

On a snowy December morning in 2001, the world in Hayward, Wisconsin, was a blanket of white. Over three feet of snow had fallen overnight in a freak storm, covering the entire town and shutting down the streets. School was canceled, and two teenagers, Alex and Chad, found themselves at the local park, their breaths misting in the cold air.

"Man, what do we do now?" Chad said, kicking at the snow.

"Snowball fight?" Alex suggested with a mischievous grin.

And just like that, they were lobbing snowballs at each other, laughter echoing in the still air. That's when a stray snowball flew past and accidentally hit a boy, Sam, attempting to walk his dog through piles of snow.

"Hey!" Sam exclaimed, half annoyed, half amused. He scooped up a handful of snow, shaping it into a perfect snowball, and threw it back. Bear, a fluffy Tibetan Mastiff, barked excitedly and darted into the snow.

From a nearby house, a curious woman, Diana, watched the unfolding scene. She smiled and called out to her daughters, Shannon and Avery. "Girls, come on! Let's join the fun!"

Bundled in snowsuits and boots, the girls giggled as they joined the impromptu snowball fight. Neighbors peeked out of their windows, drawn by the commotion, and soon, one by one, they joined in. It wasn't just a few families; entire neighborhoods spilled out onto the snow-covered streets.

The local bakery owner came out, tossing snowballs with mitten-covered hands. The firefighters from the station down the road joined, their laughter booming. Everyone in the town, regardless of their profession, was like a little kid again, excited to hit their neighbors with a powdery sphere. School teachers, grocery store clerks, and even the mayor were there, each throwing snowballs with glee.

Old Mr. Weisner, who rarely left his house, chuckled as he watched from his porch. "Well, I'll be," he murmured. Mrs. Novotny, the local librarian, emerged with a tray of hot cocoa. "For the warriors," she said with a wink.

The snowball fight grew, laughter and cheers filling the air. It wasn't long before someone mentioned, "We might be breaking a record here!"

The local newspaper came to the scene, snapping a picture to memorialize the moment. Before they knew it, word spread, and the Associated Press picked up the story. Hayward, Wisconsin, was on the map for the world's biggest snowball fight.

Years passed, and the snowball fight became an annual tradition, growing each year. But the magic of that first fight never faded.

On the 15th anniversary, the town gathered, snowballs

ready. Alex, now a teacher in the same school that was canceled that day, stood next to Chad, his lifelong friend.

"Do you remember that day?" Chad asked.

"How could I forget?" Alex laughed. "It was the day our little town showed the world the what we're made of."

As they prepared to throw the first snowballs, a fresh layer of snow began to fall, glittering in the sunlight. It was as if the town was being wrapped in a blanket of magic, a reminder of that special day a decade ago.

"Here's to creating magic," Alex said, raising his snowball.

"And to kicking your butt!" Chad added, his voice warm with memories.

They threw their snowballs, and the air was once again filled with laughter. Hayward's tradition wasn't just about breaking records; it was about hearts coming together, year after year, under the spell of a Midwestern winter's snow.

Afterword

A Personal Note from the Author

Hi, Feel-Good Fam! Kitty here! I hope you enjoyed 'Jack and Kitty's Christmas Feel-Good Stories: Holidays in the Heart-land.' This book was inspired by a cherished childhood story of mine, which I'd like to share with you below. I hope it brings the magic of the holiday season to life for you.

* * *

The Day I Fell in Love With the North Shore in Minnesota

"Can we go home? I'm cold!!" I was a little kid, around four years old. We were outside, and I was cold, desperately cold. You see, my mom is from Jamaica and, to her, something special lay in these snow drifts. To me, with my short legs, all I could see were mountains of icy whiteness.

My mom immigrated to Minnesota when she was seventeen, in the middle of winter. From a tropical paradise to one of the coldest places on Earth. It was her first time seeing snow in real life, a first among many.

You see, Jamaica is in the Caribbean and doesn't get snow. It's warm, beautiful.

Paradise.

White sand beaches and jerk chicken. A place where you can get lost in the tropical heat, where the water drifts lazily onto your toes and the sun kisses your skin. A place where you can sway to the rhythm of Bob Marley's music as the wind entices you to move your hips with the rhythms of the islands.

It's Jamaica, Mon. No worries. No cares. That's where my mom came from.

Paradise.

And here I was with her now, four years old, fighting off the bitter cold of Northern Minnesota. The wind snapped at my face, smacking me into alertness. My mom zipped my warm winter jacket all the way up to my chin and pulled my hat down to my eyebrows.

"Look," she said. "Feel," she whispered.

We had just come back from a winter vacation in Jamaica over Christmas time, and I wasn't in any mood to "look" or "feel" anything... except the warmth of my bed. Instead, all I "felt" was the pinch of frost nipping at my nose, and my belly grumbling for some hot chocolate and warm sugar cookies.

She said it again, and this time I listened. My mind raced to find the quickest path to a warm beverage and some yummy food. "Look. *Feel*."

So I looked around. Unimpressed.

Miles upon miles of white snowdrifts. Powdery layers of

glimmering jewels as far as my eyes could see. The trees were tall and untouched. It looked as if another human hadn't been here in ages.

Or ever.

Patterns of sharp edges and swirls had been formed by the elements, but to my eyes, it looked like God had been sketching on a notebook, carefully crafting a pretty mosaic for all of the animals and spirits who live here.

I looked around some more, this time noticing details I hadn't appreciated at first. A tiny brown bird, hopping on a branch, sending a mini avalanche of snow to the ground with each bounce. The wind, singing a sacred song that it had sung long before we were here, howling like a wolf for anyone who perked their ears up. The sun, dancing across the crystalline white expanse, causing the earth below my feet to literally glow.

My mom grabbed my hand, squeezed it tight in my mitten, and asked me to try even harder this time.

"Feel."

It was whispered, almost like a prayer, reverent and soft. I closed my eyes this time, somehow knowing her request had nothing to do with looking around at my surroundings but, instead, to feel what it was doing to me inside.

This place was affecting me, changing the way I felt in my gut. A warmth began to creep up, flushing my cheeks and making me want to laugh. The corners of my little mouth rose as I felt something that couldn't be described other than feeling *good*.

The rhythm of the North Woods. The song of the snow. The dance of the sun.

The realization of a little girl who had come from the carefree melodies of Jamaica, from reggae and roots, to a different song, wrapped up in snow and cold. But somehow just as warm.

The North Shore of Minnesota. Grand Marais.

Just a two-hour drive up from Duluth, the upper end of the North Shore is one of the most cherished places among Minnesota locals, and there's a good reason why. It's one of the last frontiers in the lower 48, or at least it feels that way.

You can wander off into the vast expanses of wilderness - which in most places, are only a few city blocks worth of trekking - and feel like you have reached the end of the world.

Or the beginning of it.

The air is crisp and clean here, and somehow makes you feel as if it's purifying your very lungs with every intake through your nostrils. The sun shines more brilliantly here, especially in winter. It heightens the snow's brightness, painting it in golden tones amidst the blues and whites. And the trees stand tall and proud, majestic and unforgiving.

You're in their domain, and they know that once you've had a hearty taste of this magical place - this vast expanse only a few miles from the Canadian border - you'll come back again and again for more.

This place, this land, this uncharted expanse will call your name and make you feel as if you've been transported to another place and time in history. Here, you can be George Vancouver, exploring Alaska with a sense of giddy adventure. You can be an Indigenous American, long before any unfamiliar faces showed up, knocking at your door.

You can be a daredevil, seeing how hard you can push your body, how rigorously you can hike the cliffs and towering shores that line the scenic lakes peppered throughout these lands.

You can be a family, enjoying a cozy day in front of a fire after returning from a peaceful cross-country ski or snowshoe jaunt.

Or you can be me. Four years old. Young and impressionable, ready to have my socks knocked off by the beauty of one of the last remote places that isn't truly remote.

Ready to *feel*. Ready to fall in love. Ready to return year after year because it's one of those memories your brain and heart can't shake, no matter how old you get.

The North Shore of Minnesota will *do* something to you like that. It will grip your heart and refuse to let go, carving a space in your lifelong memories that you revisit time and time again. It will paint your dreams at night, and revisit in the most unlikely places, time and time again.

It will feel like your first love. Just like it did for me, at the tender age of four years old. It will make you feel. Fall in love. Yearn to return to its warm embrace time and time again.

Do me a favor, will you?

Close your eyes, take a deep breath in. Allow yourself to imagine a place where it feels like you're four years old, discovering something you love, for the very first time. Allow me to take your hand.

Do you feel it? The warmth of my skin, the soft creases in my palm as it melds with yours?

Take a deep breath and close your eyes.

Feel.

And then, when you feel connected to the magic of this new place, open your eyes. Do you feel the excitement starting to quicken your heart, just the tiniest bit?

Christmastime amidst a sanctuary of snow warms your heart. It's like wearing a cozy sweater on a cold day. It just feels good. I hope, as you read this book, you found that magic too. The moment your heart connects with a place it can't forget.

Did you feel the warmth in your belly, the smile on your lips? I hope so. Thank you for reading this book and joining me on this journey. Hopefully, it made you fall in love with the magic of Christmas in the Heartland. And with the friendly hearts and faces that make it a place Jack and I proudly call 'home.'

Love,
Kitty (and Jack) Norton
Winona, Minnesota

Chapter 44

About the Authors

Jack and Kitty Norton are Emmy Award winning authors and Midwest travel experts. They have spent a lifetime on the road: as traveling musicians, documentary filmmakers and television producers.

They now focus on building the "Travel with Jack and Kitty" brand which includes a travel blog, guidebooks, podcast and videos. Jack and Kitty offer travelers fun and quirky things to do in Minnesota and the Midwest.

With their branded book series, "Jack and Kitty's Feel-

Good Stories" they present heartwarming tales from the heartland of America.

High school sweethearts turned married soulmates, the fun-loving couple lives in the small college town of Winona, Minnesota and would love to have you over for some tater tot hotdish.

Chapter 45

Connect with Jack and Kitty

Want FREE Stories? Join the Feel-Good Fam!

Sign up for our mailing list and receive free heartwarming stories every week in your inbox.

For more info, visit:
https://jackandkitty.com/feelgood/

* * *

Visiting the heartland of America? We have a fun travel blog and daily podcast celebrating the BEST of the Midwest!

For more info, visit:
https://jackandkitty.com/

* * *

Jack Norton & Kitty Norton

Wanna write us, email us, or be our friend? Awesome! We'd
love to connect with you.

Jack and Kitty
278 Mankato Ave, Suite 103
Winona, MN 55987
United States

Email
jackandkittyxo@gmail.com

Website
https://jackandkitty.com/

YouTube Channel
https://www.youtube.com/c/JackAndKitty

Facebook Group
https://www.facebook.com/groups/midwesttravelwith
jackandkitty

Facebook Page
https://www.facebook.com/jackandkittyxo

Instagram
https://www.instagram.com/jackandkittyxo/

TikTok
https://www.tiktok.com/@jackandkitty.com

* * *